With a strange sense that fantasy and reality had just become inextricably entwined, Amy felt her heart almost forget how to beat.

It felt almost as if she was turning in slow motion, until she finally faced the man who'd been standing behind her.

There was a weird feeling of inevitability as she looked up into those newly familiar dark eyes, but it wasn't until she caught sight of that sleek dark hair, cut close to his head when once it had curled rebelliously almost to his shoulders, that the pieces fell into place.

Zach was a *doctor*? In *her* hospital?

Josie Metcalfe lives in Cornwall with her long-suffering husband. They have four children. When she was an army brat, frequently on the move, books became the only friends that came with her wherever she went. Now that she writes them herself she is making new friends, and hates saying goodbye at the end of a book—but there are always more characters in her head, clamouring for attention until she can't wait to tell their stories.

Recent titles by the same author:

HER LONGED-FOR FAMILY*
HIS LONGED-FOR BABY*
HIS UNEXPECTED CHILD*
LIKE DOCTOR, LIKE SON

*The ffrench Doctors

A VERY SPECIAL PROPOSAL

BY
JOSIE METCALFE

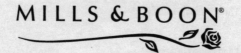

First published in Great Britain 2006
Harlequin Mills & Boon Limited,
Eton House, 18-24 Paradise Road, Richmond, Surrey TW9 1SR

© Josie Metcalfe 2006

ISBN-13: 978 0 263 84772 7
ISBN-10:   0 263 84772 1

Set in Times Roman 10½ on 12¾ pt
03-1206-51421

Printed and bound in Spain
by Litografia Rosés, S.A., Barcelona

A VERY SPECIAL PROPOSAL

CHAPTER ONE

'DID you see that programme on TV last night?' Amy heard one of the junior nurses ask her friend as they chatted together during their break. 'It was all about these people who had gone on the internet to look up their old friends and class-mates.'

'I caught part of it,' her friend agreed. 'The bit when they were saying how many marriages were ruined by people meeting up with their first loves.'

'I can't imagine having that problem with *my* first love,' the first voice said with a laugh. 'He was called Alex... something-or-other. I think he stopped growing any taller when he got to twelve—just when I started to put on a growth spurt. By the time we left school, I was head and shoulders above him even though he weighed twice as much as me.'

'Perhaps it was kissing you that stunted his growth?' teased a third voice, but, although she was smiling at their nonsense, Amy tuned out their conversation at that point, suddenly won-dering how many of *her* old classmates were still around the area. She certainly hadn't kept in touch with any of them, not once she'd left to go to medical school, and then she'd married Edward and their lives had been far too full of work-related social events—chances for her ambitious husband to 'network' with the movers and shakers in cardiothoracic surgery—to have had time to keep up with the people she'd known at school.

It had only been fairly recently that she'd returned to the area, after she'd lost Edward, and she hadn't really been interested in looking up old acquaintances…hadn't been interested in any sort of social life at all, if she was really honest.

Would any of the people she'd once known have signed up with one of those internet sites—presuming she ever worked out how to get into them? Her intermittent use of the internet was usually reserved for the same few sites devoted to medical matters, researching protocols for emergency treatment and checking the most recent drugs and their efficacy and contra-indications.

Anyway, even when she *had* lived in the area she hadn't known many people; even her classmates. She'd spent her last three years at school with her nose pressed firmly in her study books, determined to win a place at medical school. She'd allowed herself absolutely no time to think about boyfriends or…

Liar! a little voice in the back of her head accused. There *had* been one boy…young man, really, at nearly eighteen years of age…who'd done more than catch her eye.

'*Zachary Bowman,*' she whispered under cover of the surrounding chatter. She felt the same twist of guilty pleasure deep inside that had scared her so much when they'd been teenagers assigned to the same bench in the science labs. It had happened every time she'd seen his profile outlined against the tall stark windows or had dared to meet his serious dark gaze…even when their elbows or shoulders had brushed innocently as they'd reached for a flask of reagent during an experiment or noting down their findings.

He'd been every teenage girl's fantasy of 'tall, dark and handsome' with an extra dash of 'dangerous' thrown in for good measure. She could still remember that his brown eyes had been so dark that they'd appeared as black as his hair, and as for that hair, it had been unruly, with a rebellious natural curl that had made her hands tingle with the urge to stroke the heavy weight of it back off his forehead to see if it was as silky as it looked.

'The forbidden romance that never was,' she murmured wryly, remembering that, apart from one notable occasion, they'd barely exchanged a word outside the classroom or the library. And *that* occasion was definitely better off being forgotten, if the heat of revisited embarrassment climbing her cheeks was any indication.

Except she'd never really forgotten him, even though so many years had passed. Sometimes, months had gone by and any thoughts of him had been buried under the everyday load of a stressful job and a relatively high-profile marriage. But, still, she'd wondered what would have happened, whether her life would have been very different if she'd only had the courage to… What was the phrase? Take a walk on the wild side?

Wild? Amy Willmott, *née* Bowes, the original overachiever?

Suddenly she had a disturbing insight into how her life must look to others and she almost laughed aloud.

In comparison with her, plain boiled rice would seem exciting.

'For heaven's sake, what's to stop you having a go at

surfing the net?' she muttered crossly. 'It's not as if anyone else is ever going to know and think any less of you.' And there would be a certain amount of satisfaction in finding out whether Zach had avoided coming to the ignominious end that their teachers had predicted.

Or would she rather remember him the way he'd been then—forever flouting school dress code in a disreputable leather jacket as he'd thrown one long lean leg over the motorbike he'd been prohibited from parking on school property, then flashing her a wicked grin before he'd flipped the visor down on his helmet and roared off down the road.

That night, in spite of the fact that she'd had an extremely busy shift at work and was totally exhausted, somehow she just couldn't sleep.

For some time she lay in the darkness and practised the relaxation and breathing techniques that had got her through her vivas unscathed, then she tried to read a light-hearted romantic novel, but the characters just couldn't hold her attention, not when the fictional hero was having to vie with her memories.

Finally, she gave in to temptation and padded through to the spare room that she'd set up as an office where her laptop sat waiting on the desk in the corner of the room.

It was amazing how easily she found the site her colleagues had been talking about and how quickly she was able to find the name of the school she'd attended, but even before she began to scroll through the list of names, her misgivings returned, full force.

'What on earth am I doing?' she demanded of the gently humming machine, her hand hovering over the mouse. One more click would take her to the names beginning with 'B' and would tell her whether Zach's name was registered. Part of her would love to know that he'd gone on to make a success of his life, but she really *didn't* want to know that anything… anything *bad* had happened to him.

Somehow that would sully the innocent passion of her memories…the soft-focus fantasy that she'd indulged in for years that, if only he'd noticed her…asked her out on just one date…he would have discovered that she was the only woman for him and they would have lived happily ever after.

Except it had all been one-sided.

They'd spent weeks as lab partners, assigned purely on the basis of their names in the register, Bowman coming directly after Bowes, so if he'd had any interest in her as even a moderately attractive female, surely he'd have said… something! Anything!

He could have suggested they had a coffee together… walked with her after a study session in the library…taken her for a ride on his fearsomely powerful bike…

Ha!

The closest he'd ever come to that had been to throw her a wicked grin before he'd roared off into the distance, leaving her gazing wistfully after him.

Even when she'd screwed up her courage to mention the school leavers' dance, he hadn't taken the hint. Instead of a blissful evening spent in his arms, she'd had to make do with a rather strained celebratory meal with her parents in an expensive restaurant, listening to the two of them rhapsodise about the glittering future that lay ahead of her. She couldn't allow herself to be side-tracked by anything, they'd insisted. All she had to do was keep her eye on where she was going. There would be plenty of time for her to have a social life once she was qualified and surrounded by people with the same aims and aspirations…other doctors, for example…

Amy deliberately shut Edward's image away, refusing to allow guilty thoughts of the husband she'd lost just over a year ago to intrude on her present dilemma.

The cursor continued to blink patiently beside Shelley Adams's name at the top of the list but it almost seemed to taunt her. Just one more click and the section on display would be replaced by the next one and she would know whether Zach's name was there, then one more click and she would see…what? A copy of that infamous school photo with his dark unruly hair defying taming and his dark eyes…those dark eyes that had followed her through her dreams for years, even into her marriage…? Or would it be a contemporary picture with his striking features blurred by weight and age and his hairline receding towards middle age?

The idea that she might find out that he was now happily married with half a dozen beautiful dark-eyed children was somehow worse than the prospect of finding out that he'd had a fatal accident on that noisy bike of his or that he'd ended up in prison, and that was totally crazy, considering the way her own life had gone.

With her parents encouraging her every step of the way, she'd accepted the place her stellar grades had secured at one of the most prestigious medical schools in the country, and immediately after she'd qualified, she'd married Edward in a fairy-tale wedding, much to their delight.

Edward Willmott, who couldn't have been less like Zach if he'd deliberately tried. Blond-haired and blue-eyed, he'd been totally focused on getting to the top of the tree in the shortest possible time, no matter what else he had to sacrifice or postpone along the way. Edward, who had died a hero in the middle of a motorway pile-up, leaving her without the child that they were always going to have *next* year, and feeling guilty that she hadn't really appreciated what she'd had until it was gone and her life was totally empty.

She'd had it all, so why should she resent the very idea of Zach finding the same fulfilment?

'No reason at all,' she said aloud as she decisively broke the connection with the internet and shut the computer down. 'And no reason whatever to look him up, especially at this time of night when I've got to be getting up in another four hours to go to work.'

She returned to bed, determined not to let her thoughts stray in his direction again, but discovered when she woke up too early, tired and out of sorts, that she hadn't had any control over where her dreams had taken her.

'So, what would have been so bad about clicking on his name and finding out once and for all?' she demanded in the noisy confines of her little car as she headed towards the hospital at least an hour earlier than necessary. She pulled up at a pedestrian crossing as an elderly lady stepped off the pavement and started to make her shaky way across the road.

'I hope your doctor's referred you for surgery on that hip,' Amy muttered under her breath, force of habit having her analysing the woman's gait even as she smiled in response to the thanks the woman mouthed. She could only imagine how much pain the poor woman was in if she was moving that gingerly, clearly needing much more help than the inadequate support of the stick she was using.

Out of the corner of her eye she caught sight of a car

looming in her rear-view mirror. When she registered just how fast he was approaching, she cringed in anticipation of the squeal of brakes that would come when he realised he had to stop for the crossing… Except he didn't brake, merely swinging out around her as casually as though he was doing nothing more than passing an unimportant vehicle parked at the side of the road.

Time seemed to stand still for several long seconds but there was a horrific inevitability in the way the other car reached the crossing just as the elderly lady emerged beyond the shelter of Amy's car right into his path, the driver apparently making no attempt to brake.

At the very last second, the elderly lady seemed to sense what was about to happen and tried to get out of the way. Unfortunately, her painful hip limited her mobility and instead of stepping back into safety, her legs crumpled beneath her and she landed on the road with a thud.

'Oh, my God!' Amy shrieked as she flung her door wide, narrowly avoiding stepping into the path of the motorbike that was drawing up beside her. Automatic reflexes had made her reach for her keys and her handbag so that even before she'd reached the frighteningly still figure she'd found her mobile phone and was tapping in the emergency number.

'Emergency. Which service do you require?' said the voice in her ear as she sank to her knees beside the elderly woman and reached out to search for a pulse.

'Ambulance and police, please,' she answered crisply. 'There's been an accident on the pedestrian crossing about a mile south of the hospital…the one almost outside the supermarket. An elderly lady. She's unconscious but she's still breathing.'

Amy had been so relieved when her fingers had detected a steady pulse, especially when the poor woman was twisted so uncomfortably. And her impact with the ground had been audible even inside Amy's car, so she had been fearing the worst…that the woman's skull had been fractured or her neck had been broken and had killed her instantly. Her obviously broken leg was almost unimportant by comparison.

There was still the possibility that either or both had happened, but for the moment her heart was still beating and she was still breathing, and if Amy could do anything to make sure that continued to happen until the ambulance arrived with all the equipment to protect her compromised systems…

'Don't move her!' ordered a deep voice, only partly muffled by the tinted visor of his helmet as he grabbed her hand and pulled it away from monitoring the thready pulse. 'If she's injured her spine, you could paralyse her.'

He flipped up his visor with his free hand and the intensity of his dark gaze meeting hers sent an unexpected jolt of awareness through her that was totally out of place when there was a vulnerable life on the ground between them.

For a moment it was as if the injured woman didn't exist. She actually saw his pupils widen as his eyes flickered over her face, his dark eyes darkening still further in the involuntary response of a potent male towards a female. His hand tightened unconsciously around hers almost as though he was staking some sort of claim…and for one moment suspended in time all she could think was that she wanted him to remove his helmet so she could see what the rest of his face looked like.

Mortified, she closed her own eyes for a second, reminding herself sternly that this definitely wasn't the time for age-old courtship preliminaries, even if she *had* been interested in starting a relationship.

'I know not to move her,' Amy said in a voice that trembled just a bit as she retrieved her hand from his gauntleted grasp and returned gentle fingers to the wrinkled skin of the exposed throat. Under that powerful gaze she was finding it unexpectedly difficult to concentrate on explaining what she was doing, even as she silently blessed the television programmes that were educating the general population in emergency lifesaving protocols. 'I'm a doctor but I'm only monitoring her pulse and respiration until the emergency services get here.'

As if on cue, she heard the sound of approaching sirens.

'Hear that? They'll be here in a second and they'll have oxygen on board and a collar to protect her neck while they put her on a backboard to support her spine,' she explained, then couldn't help risking another glance in his direction, only to find that he was still looking at her rather than the victim.

This time the inappropriate shiver of awareness was so strong that she was afraid that he'd see it.

What on earth was going on here? She'd never reacted this way when a man looked at her, not even Edward. In fact, the only person who had been able to make her respond like this…to be aware of every molecule in her body that made her female…had been Zach.

And that was ridiculous.

Obviously, the only reason she'd thought about *him*—and the way he'd made her feel all those years ago—was because of that stupid conversation about those internet sites and her aborted search last night.

And now this man, with eyes every bit as dark as Zach's had been, was stirring things inside her that were best left sleeping, especially when she should be concentrating on the unconscious woman under her fingertips.

'Hey, Doc, have you started coming out looking for work?' teased the paramedic as he reached her side. 'Are you trying to do us out of a job?'

'Just holding the fort while you get your act together, Harry,' she retorted with a smile for the familiar face as she shifted across to give him access to their patient. 'Her breathing is obviously being impaired by the position of her head and neck but although it's rather fast, her pulse is surprisingly strong. She was just about to be run over and tried to step back too quickly on a leg that looked as if it already urgently needed a hip replacement. She just sort of crumpled to the ground and hit her head with a dreadful thump.'

At Harry's suggestion, she took over setting up IV access to save time while he selected the rest of the equipment he'd need, and then she took responsibility for holding the woman's head perfectly still while he carefully positioned the collar to protect the woman's spinal cord. Then they were going to have to straighten her limbs before they could put her on the backboard, checking for breaks and compromised circulation at every stage before they could log-roll her onto it and load her into the ambulance for transportation. Silently, she was worried that the poor woman could easily slip into a coma after such an accident, but it was also a mercy that she was too deeply unconscious to be aware of the pain of her injuries.

Over the paramedic's shoulder she saw one young policeman trying to impose some sort of order on the rapidly developing traffic chaos while another was scribbling furiously into his notebook as the motorcyclist spoke to him.

His helmet was now propped on one hip, discarded leather gauntlets inside and held in position by an apparently non-chalant arm that ended in a knotted fist that seemed to give mute evidence to his underlying impatience with bureaucratic niceties—or was it an indication of his anger at the callous disregard of the driver who had caused the tragedy?

Amy regretted the fact that his back was turned towards her so that she couldn't see his face. Not that the back view was anything to sniff at, all long lean legs and narrow waist topped by broad shoulders. Disappointingly, after her memories of Zach, the sleek dark hair was cut close to the owner's head.

Zach's had been quite a bit longer, far too long to satisfy school rules, and the natural curl in it had made it unruly and tempting and…and what on earth was the matter with her? She was in the middle of the road, holding the head of an injured woman, and one false move on her part could paralyse her if she'd fractured bones in her neck. What on earth was she doing, ogling a motorcyclist she'd never seen in her life before and thinking about a classmate she hadn't seen in more than a decade? *Concentrate!* she berated herself.

She joined Harry in a sigh of relief when the collar was successfully secured and had to stifle another sigh as she wondered how much longer it would be before she felt free to go to work. Doubtless, she would have to give her statement, too, and her colleagues wouldn't be pleased if they had to wait hours for her to arrive before they could hand over and clock off at the end of a long shift. None of them would dream of walking out of the department, knowing that their departure would leave it understaffed, but they wouldn't be happy if they had to stay on indefinitely, especially those with families waiting for them to come home.

As if he'd heard her thoughts, the young officer smiled in her direction and called, 'Would it be better if I caught up with you at the hospital, Doctor?'

'Perfect!' Amy called back, knowing he would be able to see her relief in her answering smile. She might actually be able to get to work on time if she didn't have to stop to answer questions now. 'I'm Dr Willmott. Amy Willmott, and I work in A and E.'

Then she bent towards the fragile lady to help slide the backboard gently into position on the wheeled stretcher, hoping that the motorcyclist wouldn't see her blush and guess at the cause. It was certainly the most blatant she'd ever been, deliberately announcing who she was and where he could contact her if he was as interested as his dark eyes had implied.

'Thanks for your assistance,' Harry said as he finally locked one door shut then climbed into the back of the ambulance to join his patient. 'I'll probably see you again in a minute, if you're on duty?'

Amy glanced at her watch and grimaced.

'I'm due to clock on in about six and a half minutes, so I'll see you there,' she confirmed as she reached in her pocket for her keys.

She hurried towards her car, still sitting in front of the pedestrian crossing where she'd left it, although someone had sensibly closed the door so it wasn't causing quite so much of an obstruction.

Her heart sank when she realised that the motorcycle was

no longer beside it. She had to fight the urge to look around for its owner, even though she knew it was crazy to expect him to hang about at the site of an accident just for a chance to speak to her again, then she heard a heavy engine being kick-started into life nearby and her pulse rate soared.

Unable to help herself, she cast a quick glance across, her eyes finding him at the side of the road just in time to see him finish pulling his helmet on over that sleek dark hair while the engine rumbled powerfully between his thighs.

'Drat!' she muttered crossly as she fastened her seat-belt, realising that she'd only just missed her chance to see his face.

As she set her car in gear and threaded her way through the tangle of vehicles and strobe-type lights ringing the accident site, she had to suppress the old pang of regret that she'd never been brave enough to ask Zach to take her for a ride on his bike. She'd wanted to, desperately. She'd even dreamed about it, imagining how it would feel to have her hair flying out behind her as they outraced the throaty roar of the engine with her arms wrapped tightly around his lean waist and her head pressed against his shoulder...

'Just another fantasy, of course,' she muttered wryly as she manoeuvred her car into a tiny corner space left near the light that would illuminate this part of the staff car park as soon as dusk came. She wriggled out of the door that was so close to the next car that it could only open halfway, grateful that she was still slim enough to do it, and set off at a brisk walk towards the main entrance to the hospital. 'The reality would probably have been very different,' she scolded herself. 'My ears would have got so cold that they made my teeth ache and I'd have got a collection of dead flies in my teeth and up my nose.'

'You made it, Amy, girl,' said a softly accented voice as she arrived at the admissions desk, her belongings hastily stuffed in her locker and a white coat pulled on over her clothes to try to disguise the grubby scuffs that had appeared on the knees of her trousers.

'With a minute and a half to spare, Louella,' Amy pointed out to the colleague waiting to hand over and get back home to her children before they had to leave for school. 'I would have been here earlier, but there was an accident—'

'On the crossing by the supermarket,' Louella finished for her. 'Yes, Harry told us when he brought her in. He told us it wasn't *his* fault if you were late because you'd volunteered to hold his hand.'

'As if!' Amy scoffed. They both knew that Harry was a very happily married man whose paramedic expertise didn't need any hand-holding either. 'Who's looking after the lady he brought in?'

'Ben Finchley and the new guy starting today.'

Ben was one of the best in the department so she didn't have to worry that her little lady was getting anything but first-class treatment.

'New guy? Remind me,' she demanded as she cast an eye over the multicoloured annotations on the grid of the white-board and stifled a groan at the sheer number of patients waiting for attention. 'I hope he's not someone still wet behind the ears or we'll never get through this lot.'

'Hardly!' Louella exclaimed as she signed off on the last of the patients she'd treated with a flourish. 'Apparently, he's just finished a six-month stint in a huge A and E somewhere in Africa. I think it might have been that big hospital in Johannesburg.'

Amy blinked in surprise at the information, then wondered with her usual feeling of uneasiness if he was one of the doctors who'd been lured to Britain to prop up the ailing health service. When were the bean counters ever going to realise that it would be far more economic to retain their own staff by paying them properly, rather than robbing the rest of the world of their indigenous and desperately needed medical staff.

But there was no point voicing her thoughts here, in an A and E department that was frequently rushed off its feet. She'd be preaching to the converted, both about the effect of poor levels of pay on staff retention and their general dislike of poaching staff from other countries.

'So, you think he's going to be worth having on staff?'

'Even if he isn't able to pull his weight, he'll be worth having around,' Louella said with a decidedly lascivious grin. 'He's definitely what the kids would call eye candy!'

'Louella! What would Sam think if he heard you talking like that?' Amy chided with a spurt of laughter. Life was never dull with Louella around.

'Sam knows I'm married, not dead!' the Caribbean woman declared robustly. 'And he knows I've got good taste because I chose him! Now, let me tell you what you've got waiting for you, then you have a good day, girl, and don't get up to too much mischief.' A few minutes later, the relevant information listed, she blew Amy a jaunty kiss as she bustled eagerly out of the department, clearly anticipating the welcome waiting for her at home.

For just a second, the lack of anything like a welcoming family in her own home made Amy aware that her life wasn't quite as perfect as she liked to pretend, but there were too many patients waiting for attention for her to spend any more time bewailing the things she didn't have any more. She had her health and a satisfying job, she reasoned as she reached for the first file, and that was more than many could boast.

She'd dealt with more than half a dozen assorted cases before she caught up with Ben Finchley as he came out of one of the treatment rooms.

'Hey, Ben, what happened to that little lady? Broken leg and head impact first thing this morning?' she demanded, thoughts of the poor woman having haunted her ever since the ambulance had whisked her away from the scene of the accident. 'Were you able to do anything for her, or…?'

'You mean Ruth?' he said with a chuckle that shocked Amy. The woman had looked so fragile that she'd been trying to prepare herself for a worst-case scenario all morning, certainly not laughter. 'If ever there was a case of being fooled by first appearances, it was that little lady,' Ben said, gesturing towards the staffroom then walking beside her as she took the hint that she looked as if she was overdue for a break. 'She looked so frail that we were convinced she must have shattered half of the bones in her body, but when we X-rayed, the only major things we could find wrong were a broken femur and a collection of spectacular bruises.'

'But…' Amy blinked. 'Are you sure we're talking about the same patient? You can't mean the woman who had to throw herself backwards to avoid being run over. Her legs collapsed under her and she hit the ground so *hard*…'

'The very same,' Ben confirmed with a broad grin. 'Like you, we were convinced we were going to find a fractured skull, at the very least, and we were half expecting her to peg out before we could do anything for her. Instead, she's already conscious and it looks as if she's going to pull through and come out of it with colours flying, once the orthopods patch her leg up with a shiny new joint.' He lifted the jar of coffee and a questioning eyebrow and Amy nodded, still bemused by the incredible tale he was telling.

'Mind you,' he continued, as he poured in the hot water and added a splash of milk to each when she nodded again, 'that doesn't mean that she hasn't got the mother and father of all headaches at the moment, but when we tried to give her some morphine to take some of the pain away while she waited to go to Theatre, she told us in no uncertain terms that she didn't want any of that nasty stuff because it made her sick the last time she was given it—when she had her appendix taken out as a teenager.'

He turned to hand her the steaming mug and offer her a giant glass jar of sugar when he caught sight of someone over Amy's shoulder. 'Hey, here's the man who was working on Ruth with me. Have you met our new colleague? He's just joined us from a hospital on the other side of the world where the sort of thing we deal with here would be nothing more than a walk in the park. Amy Willmott, meet Zach Bowman.'

CHAPTER TWO

WITH a strange sense that fantasy and reality had just become inextricably entwined, Amy's heart almost forgot how to beat.

It felt almost as if she was turning in slow motion until she finally faced the man who'd been standing behind her.

There was a weird feeling of inevitability as she looked up into those newly familiar dark eyes but it wasn't until she caught sight of that sleek dark hair cut close to his head, when once it had curled rebelliously almost to his shoulders, that the pieces fell into place.

'It was *you!*' she breathed when she recognised the motorcyclist from the scene of the accident that morning, the broad shoulders she'd admired earlier in the day so much wider and more muscular than those of the teenage boy she remembered so clearly. 'Why didn't you say something?'

'It wasn't the time or the place and, anyway, I didn't know if you'd even remember me,' he said, then she caught a glimpse of that old familiar gleam in his eyes. 'So, ABC, how have you been?'

'*ABC?* Do you two know each other already?' Ben was trying to keep up with this unexpected development but Amy barely heard him, every atom of her concentration focused on the man she'd nearly looked up on the internet just last night, the man she'd been convinced that she'd never see again because he was probably in prison or dead. Zach was a *doctor*? In *her* hospital?

'Amy Bowes Clark was my lab partner for sciences when we were at school together,' Zach explained with a slightly dismissive air, as though the matter was hardly worth mentioning, and Amy was struck by a pang that felt almost like disappointment.

'You know very well that I never used the Clark, *and* I regretted ever telling you about it,' she added crisply, remembering the way it had given him ammunition for teasing her about being far too upper crust for an ordinary state school. But at the same time it had also caused a strange sense of connection with him that he'd actually felt at ease enough with her to tease her about her family name and what it did to her initials. It had been more than he ever had with the other members of their class.

'Dr Bowman?' called a voice from the door, and all three of them turned to see one of the younger receptionists there. Her eyes were bright with appreciation as they travelled over Zach's lean frame and Amy was startled to feel the sharp claws of possessive jealousy rake her when he smiled back at the young woman.

'The police just phoned through and I thought you'd like to get the message as soon as possible,' she said with an ingratiating smile that clearly telegraphed her availability. 'They said to tell you that they ran that licence plate you gave them, and they've tracked the car down. They found clear evidence that it had been involved in a recent accident and wanted to know if it could have struck the patient. They'll want to compare DNA from your patient.'

'Did they leave a contact number?'

'Oh, yes! Here,' she purred as she offered him a piece of paper, then added in a blatant attempt at seduction, 'And I put my number on there, too…in case you needed it for…anything.'

'Thank you for passing the message on so promptly,' Zach said blandly, tucking the piece of paper in his pocket unread. He turned to Ben and Amy. 'What are the protocols in the hospital for getting permission for taking DNA samples?'

There was a silence that went on just a beat or two too long as the woman left the room, clearly crestfallen that Zach hadn't responded to her invitation with something more personal, but as soon as the door closed behind her there was a definite response from the rest of the males in the room.

'Hey! You're in there, Zach!' called one.

'Way to go!' hooted another. 'That's quick work.'

'You haven't even been here for a day and they're already panting after you. You'll have to tell us your secret,' said a third.

'It's probably just that I'm new,' Zach said dismissively, and when Amy saw the darker colour seeping over the lean planes of his face she suddenly realised that he was genuinely uncomfortable with the attention.

'It always happens with fresh meat, male or female, or can't you remember that far back, John?' she teased one of the older consultants who'd joined in the catcalls. 'Give it a day or two for her to see him haggard and unshaven at the end of a long shift and she'll soon turn her sights on someone else.'

'Now I don't know whether to thank you for taking the

heat off me or feel insulted that you were so dismissive of my charms,' Zach said so softly that his voice probably didn't reach even as far as Ben's ears.

He'd leaned closer to her, close enough for her to see every one of those absurdly long eyelashes and the start of creases at the corners of his eyes put there, in all probability, by six months of squinting into fierce African sunlight. He was also close enough for her to be able to feel the warmth emanating from his body and smell the hint of soap or shampoo that still lingered on his skin in spite of several hours of hard and often messy work.

It wasn't anything with a strong perfume—she couldn't ever remember him smelling of anything other than plain clean soap and water—and when it was underscored by the individual musky scent of his skin, it made her body react more strongly than Edward's expensive colognes ever had.

His raised eyebrow reminded her that she hadn't replied to his last comment but her brain was so overloaded with his proximity that she couldn't even remember what he'd said.

Luckily, her blushes were spared by a head appearing around the door to announce the imminent arrival of several ambulances and she was left with the choice of scalding her mouth, trying to finish her coffee too fast, or abandoning the mug. She abandoned it with one last longing look and a mental note to try again soon. Her brain would soon slow down if she became dehydrated.

The brain is a perverse thing, she mused an hour later as she ducked a flailing fist as she tried to position an IV.

The patient on the table was suffering from multiple injuries from a car crash, yet, in spite of the fact he desperately needed their help, insisted in trying to fight them off.

Her own brain was no more logical.

Her first response to having to leave Zach to get to work on the unending influx of patients was relief. But, at the same time, her brain seemed to be silently counting the seconds until she could see him again, desperate to know whether her initial reaction to his presence had just been the result of shock.

It *must* be, she told herself reassuringly. It couldn't be anything more than a knee-jerk reaction to meeting the man she'd been thinking about just last night. She'd got over that silly crush years ago.

Really? taunted the voice inside her head. *Then why are your eyes searching him out every time you walk to your next patient and why are you straining your ears for the sound of his voice?*

'That's just because…because I want a chance to find out what happened to turn his life around,' she justified defiantly under her breath as she pulled on a second pair of gloves to treat one of the department's 'regulars'—a young drug addict whose HIV had already developed into full-blown AIDS.

'What happened this time, Tommy?' she asked gently as she took in the battered face. The way he was hunched over with his arms wrapped protectively around his ribs told her that they were probably in the same state.

'Some people don't seem to like beggars,' he mumbled painfully through split lips.

'*I* think you just can't stay away from me,' she teased as she slowly helped him to take off the clothing hanging on his skeletal frame, hoping she wouldn't find anything more than bruises. She didn't know whether he had enough reserves in his system to cope with broken ribs or, even worse, a punctured lung.

'Sorry, Doc. You aren't my type,' he retorted with an attempt at a smile that ended in a wince as he opened up the cut on his lip again. 'On the other hand, *that* is someone I could *really* go for…' There was an unexpected gleam of appreciation in his least swollen eye as he nodded at something he could see beyond her shoulder.

Amy turned to find out who had caught his eye, and there, through a gap in the curtains, was Zach, a quizzical expression on his face as he watched…what? Tommy? Her?

Their eyes met and when her heart felt as if it turned a complete somersault in her chest she realised that this was something more than the lingering memory of a teenage crush.

'You and me both,' she muttered with feeling, and her hands tingled with more than a remembered longing to explore the clean lines of his face and the strength of his powerful body.

Tommy laughed aloud. 'Down, girl!' he teased as Zach responded to the sudden burst of sound, his dark eyes seeming to find hers unerringly. 'It wouldn't be a fair contest…I'm in no condition to fight you for him.'

The reminder that the young man was her patient and had potentially serious injuries snapped her back to what she should be doing with a guilty start, but she still had to force herself to drag her eyes away from the man outside the curtain.

'So, let's see what we can do to get you back in fighting form,' she suggested, and began to palpate the darkly bruised ribs.

'I dunno about fighting form,' he said around a groan of pain. 'I'd be grateful just to have a good summer. I'd rather not be around when winter comes.'

'What do you mean?' she asked, concerned. There had been such resignation in his tone…far too much for someone who hadn't even reached his twenties yet.

'I won't make it through another winter on the street,' he said bluntly. 'And to tell the truth, I don't really want to.'

'Oh, Tommy… If you had a place in a hostel…' Amy began, but he was shaking his head before she could complete the sentence.

'They'll only take you in if you're clean—off drugs,' he clarified, in case she didn't understand.

'But I'm sure we could find you a place on a programme to—'

'Not a lot of point, is there, Doc, with me in this state? Anyway, I'm not too keen on going back into the system, seeing as how it was the system that did this to me.'

'I don't understand,' she said quietly while she systematically cleaned up his wounds one by one, taping steristrips over the cuts that would heal without stitches and leaving the worst until last for suturing. This was the most she'd ever heard Tommy say about his life but she'd known that there were dark shadows in his background—she could tell by the expression in his eyes. They held the same fathomless, wary depths that she'd first seen in…Zach?

'I was put into care when I was about four, when my mum dumped me at the social services office, and the system was so glad they'd found somewhere to put me that they forgot about me.'

He fixed her with eyes that were uncannily like Zach's for the amount they kept hidden, but suddenly she realised that there was also a banked inferno of emotions raging underneath his apparent apathy.

'By the time someone thought to check up on *why* I kept trying to run away, the bastard who was supposed to be looking after me like a father had been abusing me for years and I was HIV positive.'

'Oh, Tommy…' Amy breathed, her heart breaking for all the misery he'd suffered in his life…was still suffering, she realised, confronted with the evidence of his latest assault.

'Hey, I'm cool,' he said with an awkward shrug, even though the slight flush of colour in his pale cheeks told her he'd been touched by her sympathy. 'If I'm lucky, it'll be a good summer. I've got no job to go to so I'll be outside in the sunshine with plenty of time to listen to the birds and smell the flowers while I stick my hand out for money for my next fix. By the time winter comes…who knows?' he finished with another shrug and a corresponding grunt of pain when the manoeuvre jarred his ribs.

'Have you been taking any anti-retroviral medications?' Even as she asked, Amy realised that Tommy's drug abuse would probably preclude his adherence to any regular preventative treatment.

'Nah,' he said dismissively, obeying her silent gesture to turn his head for the next set of stitches to close the wound in his scalp. 'They made me feel worse than coming off dope, and it was already too late to have any real effect. Anyway, if I was given a supply of drugs…any drugs…I'd more than likely be mugged for them.'

Amy couldn't argue with that. Tommy was the expert when it came to conditions on the streets.

'Well, you probably already know that one of the dangers now is developing an infection that your body can't fight.'

'So they tell me, but I've been lucky so far—apart from

having the crap kicked out of me. Haven't had anything more than a cold.'

The conversation died for a few minutes while Amy concentrated on making a neat job of his scalp, grateful that he'd chosen such a brutally short hairstyle as it made the task so much easier.

Finally, as she handed over to the nurse to tape a protective dressing in place, she positioned herself so that she met his gaze head on, her pen poised over the clipboard that held his notes.

'So, Tommy, if I give you a course of antibiotics, will you promise me that you'll take the whole course?'

'How long is a course?' he parried warily.

'Just until you come back to have your stitches taken out?' she bargained, her heart aching that there was so little she could do for him. 'A week? Would you be able to keep them out of sight for a week?'

'Make it five days and I'll do my best,' he countered, then grinned cheekily. 'And that's only because you asked nicely.'

'They break your heart sometimes, the way they've had to survive,' said a quiet voice just behind her, and when Amy looked over her shoulder and up into Zach's dark eyes she realised that he understood far more about the hell Tommy had gone through than she would ever know.

'So, who is *Mr* Willmott?' said that same voice right behind her in the cafeteria queue, and Amy gasped, dragged out of her pessimistic thoughts about young Tommy's chances of surviving into his twenties by the man who could have ended up just like Tommy, if his teachers had been right.

'*Dr* Willmott,' she corrected automatically, only remembering as she said it that, of course, it had reverted to Mr when Edward had climbed up the next rung of the promotion ladder. Not that it was relevant any more.

'Really,' Zach said as he took a tray from the pile and kept pace with her slow shuffle in the queue towards the hot meals. 'I presume he works here. Is he in A and E, too, or one of the other departments?'

'No, he doesn't work here.' Suddenly she felt strangely guilty to be talking about her husband with Zach, but couldn't find a way to end the conversation without sounding rude. 'He's… He was killed. A year ago. On the motorway.'

The words emerged in jerky lumps. Uncomfortable. Unpractised.

After the initial 'getting to know you' enquiries, the other A and E staff had tactfully refrained from asking for any more painful details and she certainly hadn't volunteered. The only people who talked about Edward any more were her parents, bewailing the loss of her handsome, successful husband every time she set foot in their house, and his parents, endlessly, when she made her duty visits.

And yet…for the first time, she actually *wanted* to talk about what had happened. Did this mean that she was actually coming to terms with her loss, or was it because it was Zach she was telling?

Almost as soon as they were sitting down she found the stark details pouring out of her as if she needed to purge herself of the words. Somehow, in spite of the fact that she hadn't seen him for so many years—and hadn't really known him well even then—she knew that she could trust him with her confidences.

'There was a pile-up in bad weather…dozens of cars involved…a woman had been thrown out of a vehicle. Apparently, Edward saw it happen. He pulled over and got out to help and was hit by another car. He was killed instantly.'

'I'm sorry,' Zach said, visibly shocked and clearly at a loss for what to say.

'He was on his way back from a conference,' Amy went on, the words coming easier now that she'd started. 'I didn't even know it had happened…that he was dead…until the police came to tell me.' She shuddered at the memory of the late-night knock at the door.

'Did you have any children?' he asked, a perfectly ordinary question but one that caused a familiar pang for lost opportunities.

'No. We hadn't got as far as starting a family,' she admitted sadly. 'It's still just me and my parents.'

For a second she thought she saw something dark in his eyes at that information, but couldn't be sure—it was gone too soon.

She knew it couldn't have been put there by her mention of her family, because he'd never met them, but that didn't stop her speculating that she might have reminded him about something painful in *his* past.

How many relationships had he had since the days when she'd sighed over him in their biology and chemistry lessons? Probably far too many to count, with his bad-boy good looks…and why the thought of all those women should cause something painful to tighten around her heart…

'Do you still live in the same place?' he asked. 'The big stone house near the top of the hill?'

'I've got my own place now, not far from the hospital, but… How did you know where I lived?'

There was a glimpse of that shadow in his eyes again but then it was gone, hidden behind those thick dark lashes that he still seemed to have a habit of using to camouflage his thoughts.

'How did I know where the princess's castle was?' he teased, looking up from the coffee he'd purchased to finish his meal, but there was an edge to his voice that was all too reminiscent of the old Zach. 'Everyone knew where the Bowes Clarks lived. It certainly wasn't any secret.'

And how Amy had hated the fact that, all too often, as soon as people realised who her parents were, they treated her differently, as though family wealth made her something other than just another teenager trying to get good exam results. Unfortunately, her parents still had some sort of crazy idea that their family was somehow inherently 'better class' than their neighbours and that their daughter should automatically—

Her thoughts were cut off by the simultaneous shrilling of their pagers.

'Well, we almost managed an uninterrupted meal,' Zach said as they both hastily piled the debris onto a single tray, depositing it in the appropriate place as they hurried towards the door, knowing that the 'multiple trauma' message could be anything from a small handful to dozens that would require all available staff.

'Sorry to interrupt your meal break,' the co-ordinator said as they appeared in the department, her gaze taking on a speculative air as she saw them arrive together. 'We're taking in the overflow from a major motorway incident. Initial estimates of ten vehicles involved seems to be going up every time the emergency services speak to us. The last person I spoke to said it could be as many as thirty.'

'So, where do you want us, Liz?' Amy offered, not envying her the major logistical nightmare she was going to have to deal with over the next few hours.

'Could you both start off processing the walking wounded to keep the decks clear for the major injuries coming in? At some stage you'll have to be redirected to Resus as the more serious patients start arriving, but—'

'Has someone warned the patients already waiting that they could be about to be pushed to the back of the list again?' Zach asked with a glance towards the grid on the whiteboard that was heavily populated with the names of the people already signed into the department and waiting for attention.

'I'm just about to do that,' the co-ordinator said with a grimace. 'I wanted to get my troops organised first.'

'Bang goes the department's performance targets,' Amy said grimly. 'Those politicians who think they can sit at a desk and tell a doctor how many minutes it should take to treat a patient should try coming down here and seeing what it's like living in the real world. It couldn't be *less* like a production line in a factory.'

'Don't get me started!' Liz warned. 'If they'd only pay the staff properly we'd have enough of them willing to stay to do the job. As it is, all the money seems to be swallowed up by employing more and more administrators to carry stop-watches for the politicians.'

'I heard that there are now more administrators in the hospital than there are patients!' offered one of the staff nurses as she moved a patient's name from one place on the board across to the list signifying that they were now waiting their turn for X-rays.

'Don't depress me!' Liz groaned with a shake of her head

as Amy hurried after Zach, her voice carrying along the corridor. 'I wouldn't mind if the extra staff were actually doing some of the real work…cleaning floors, delivering meals or spending time with patients. As it is, it seems as if their only function is to draw eye-watering salaries for shuffling unnecessary papers…'

'Oops! I'm sorry I spoke!' Amy murmured with a wry grin as she and Zach stationed themselves in adjoining stations in a three-bay treatment room, donning gloves and disposable aprons in preparation for their first patients. 'I didn't mean to set her off like that.'

'It's such a sore spot with medical personnel that it's difficult not to,' Zach said sombrely. 'When you apply to medical school, they certainly don't warn you just how demoralised you'll be by the time you finish your training. You've just spent years piling up debt while you slog your guts out to qualify, and you…*we*…can see what's wrong and how to fix it, but they bring in someone from big business who hasn't a clue what medical priorities are and he builds an empire of bean counters trying to run it like…like…'

'Perhaps *you* should think about something else, too, or your blood pressure will be astronomical,' Amy teased, even as she appreciated the fire in his eyes as he voiced his views.

They barely had time to treat one patient apiece before the floodgates opened and from that point on there certainly wasn't time to conduct a debate about the shortcomings of the health service. There *was* time, though, for Amy to realise that Zach's impassioned pronouncement showed a different side of his character to the Zach she'd known all those years ago.

Then he'd mostly kept his head down below the parapet,

limiting his subversion to the length of his hair, his leather jacket and his motorbike. Even so, the teachers had seemed to target him for scorn and derision, belittling his work in front of his peers and denigrating his chances of ever making anything of himself.

'If they could only see him now!' she breathed into her disposable mask as she hurried to lend him a hand putting in a drain when a patient collapsed spectacularly with a previously undiagnosed flail chest. Every movement was swift, decisive, accurate and, in its own way, beautiful to watch. There was absolutely nothing of the juvenile delinquent in this caring, dedicated man.

'Thanks for your help,' he said, the slightly gruff tone to his voice her only clue to the fact that he'd been worried whether he would be able to sort out the problem before it resulted in brain damage and heart failure.

'You're welcome,' she said with a smile that answered his relief, and suddenly knew that there was more to the words than their social meaning.

It had only been a matter of hours since she'd been tempted to try to track him down on an internet website. Not wanting to destroy her teenage fantasies, she'd decided against finding out what had happened to him but, as if by magic, he'd reappeared in her life.

'So, where do I go from here?' she murmured, groaning as she tried to stretch the kinks out of her neck and shoulders after long minutes spent retrieving far too much of a shattered windscreen from a child's face. It was going to take the expert techniques of their most experienced plastic surgeon to minimise the scarring that would be a permanent reminder of this day. In the meantime, she could step out of the way while the cubicle was cleared of debris and readied for the next patient and lean back against the nearest wall to allow her spinal muscles to recover. She didn't even have the energy to remove her gloves or apron.

'You're not thinking of leaving, are you?' Zach demanded, his shoulder almost touching hers as he joined her against the wall. 'I thought you were settled in the area?'

Amy blinked at the unexpected questions, belatedly realising that she must have spoken her own thoughts aloud.

What could she say? *I was just wondering whether I had any more chance of attracting you now than I did as a teenager?*

'I am settled, I think. I'm close enough to my parents so that visiting them doesn't have to be a major time-consuming trek, yet far enough away so I can call my life my own...' ...*More or less*, she added silently, hoping she hadn't grimaced at the thought of the way the two of them still tried to organise her life for her.

Which reminded her, she thought with a barely stifled groan.

There had been a message on her phone earlier, reminding her that she was supposed to be attending some 'do' this evening. She certainly couldn't remember what it was about—with her father a stalwart member of so many prestigious committees and boards of governors, there was usually *something* at which it was 'imperative' she show her face.

She also had a sneaking suspicion that, now that a year had passed since she'd been widowed, her mother was trying to be surreptitious about using the events to introduce her to a selection of 'suitable' men from whom she would be expected to choose another husband.

Not that her parents could ever find fault with her first choice, as they told her *ad nauseam*, but if she was ever to provide them with the grandchild they needed if they were to pass on their inheritance…

For just a second she toyed with the idea of inviting Zach to go as her partner, but it was definitely a less shocking idea than it would have been when he'd sported his unruly hair and an attitude to match. He might still ride a motorbike, but as a fully qualified doctor, the rebel was now well and truly part of the establishment.

Anyway, if she did ever get up the courage to invite Zach to go out with her—or vice versa—the very last place she'd want to go to fulfil her fantasy would be anywhere under her parents' eagle eyes.

She glanced up at the clock, hoping for a moment that the current workload would give her the excuse to phone and cancel, but no such luck.

'Clock-watching?' Zach asked while she was still trying to work out some way of avoiding an evening of tedium. 'Got a hot date this evening?'

'Hardly!' She laughed. 'Just a command performance at some semi-formal function—some committee or other—and the very *last* thing I want to do after a shift like this. I can't imagine anything worse than being herded into a room full of people spouting inanities, plied with white wine so acid that you could use it to clean drains and offered very pretty-looking "nibbles" that are totally tasteless unless they've been over-loaded with salt and artificial flavourings when I'd far rather have a hearty plate of spaghetti Bolognese or carbonara.'

Zach chuckled. 'I remember that about you—the way you could always put away about twice the calories of any other

woman and still stay so slim. *And* you had the best brain in
the class. No wonder the other girls were jealous of you.'

Simultaneously embarrassed by the praise and delighted
that he'd noticed anything personal about her, she forgot to
keep a tight rein on her tongue.

'*If* they were jealous of me it was because I had the sexiest
boy in the class as my lab partner,' she countered, then
groaned in humiliation, mortified that she couldn't remember
what she'd last touched with her gloved hands and so couldn't
even cover her red face. Furious with herself for putting her
foot in her own mouth, she stripped the gloves off and flung
them into the bin then made a performance about donning a
clean pair.

'The sexiest boy in the class?' he repeated with a dawning
grin. 'Really? If only I'd known!'

'You *must* have known!' she exclaimed. 'That's why you
always grew your hair so long, wore the leather jacket and
rode the motorbike…a motorbike, by the way, that everyone
in the class, male or female, wanted an invitation to ride.'

'Ready for your next one?' prompted Liz in the doorway
behind them while Amy was still desperately wanting to call
back her words. If only there was a way of turning the clock
back just one minute. 'We're down to the last few who were
delayed by the influx from the motorway.'

'Wheel them in,' Zach invited in a resigned tone that completely disappeared as soon as Liz's head did from the
doorway. Then he took several long strides to bring him close
enough that their shoulders touched as he leant against the
wall beside her, his broad muscular one against her more
slender one.

Below the short sleeves of their faded green scrubs his firm flesh was hot and darkly tanned against her cooler, paler skin, but she shivered at the intimacy of the contact, over-whelmingly aware that he was doing it deliberately.

'One day,' he murmured for her ears alone, 'I might tell you why I really dressed that way.'

CHAPTER THREE

ZACH leant back into the corner of the wooden bench, swung his feet up onto the other end of the seat and sighed with relief.

It felt as if it had been days since he'd last had time to sit down and it wasn't just his feet doing the complaining.

He took a cautious sip of the outsized mug of coffee, then a deeper draught when he found it had cooled enough on his journey out to this little courtyard area hidden in an angle of the building housing the A and E department.

His view of the night sky was disappointing. It wasn't fully dark yet, but many of the stars would always remain invisible because there were so many streetlights around.

It hadn't been like that at the refugee camp. There, when night had fallen, the only light to break the complete darkness had been the occasional flickering of firelight or the generator-powered lights in the operating theatre. There, the sky had been full of billions of points of starlight, all so clear and bright that it had seemed as if he could almost reach out and grab a handful of them.

Fanciful nonsense, of course, just like his dream last night that Amy was riding on the back of his motorbike, her arms wrapped around his waist and her body pressed tightly against him as they sped through the night together.

Had his subconscious somehow known that she was about to reappear in his life? Had it been warning him, or was it that age-old wishful thinking? If he'd known that the elegant woman bending over the elderly hit-and-run victim had been *his* ABC he might have managed to introduce himself in an adult manner. As it was, he'd had a hard time trying not to swallow his tongue as all those old feelings had flooded over him in a maelstrom.

'Ha!' he snorted into the darkness. 'Even my dreams are stuck in an adolescent time warp. You'd think I'd manage to come up with something new in the last fifteen years!'

It wasn't as if he'd received any encouragement from her, then or now. She would always be the princess to his pauper, something that was obvious even when they were both wearing unisex scrub suits. She would never look anything less than cool and elegant while he…

He glanced down at the crumpled state of the shapeless garb and chuckled at the thought of covering the top half, at least, under his leather jacket. That was the way he'd coped at school, camouflaging the fact that although they were perfectly clean, his clothes were disintegrating with age because there was so little money to replace them.

Anyway, it wasn't as though smart clothing would have made any difference at school. According to his teachers, he had been thick and stupid and on the fast track to oblivion. Amy had been the only one who'd spoken to him as if he'd had more than two brain cells between his ears. She'd been the one who'd made him think that, perhaps, there might be another road to travel than the one to perdition, that, maybe, she would be interested in him if he were to ask.

He'd soon found out that the princess's interest had been anything but personal, and for a week or two had gone into self-destruct mode. Luckily, that hadn't happened until *after* he'd taken all his exams, and by the time his successful results had come through he'd got his head on straight again and his eyes fixed on that distant goal.

'And it's staying that way!' he declared into the darkness, even as the alarm on his watch reminded him that it was time to get ready for the hospital fundraiser he'd been conned into attending.

He swung his feet to the ground and levered himself upright with a groan. 'So, just you remember that you learned your lesson the first time around,' he reminded himself sternly. 'Princesses and paupers don't mix.'

Except the reminder didn't stop his pulse rate rocketing into the stratosphere when he saw Amy enter the room an hour later, her honey hair freshly coiled in some elegant arrangement high on her head and her slender body draped in a fluid column of something dark blue shot with shimmering strands of silver that instantly made him think of stars in a midnight sky.

'Fanciful nonsense,' he muttered under his breath as he turned his back on her and accepted a glass from the brimming tray offered by a smiling waiter. But, even though he set off to circulate in the opposite direction, somehow he always seemed to know exactly where she was, the pale gold of her hair attracting his gaze like a candle flame across a dim room.

Finally, with an audible groan that startled the heavily bejewelled matron beside him, he gave in to the inevitable.

'Dr Willmott, I presume?' he said when he joined her at one side of the crowd. 'You look a little different.'

'Zach!' The pleasure in her eyes when she caught sight of him gave his spirits a nitroglycerine lift, as did the subtle widening of her pupils when her eyes travelled over his evening suit. 'You scrub up well, too. I've never met a man yet who didn't look good in a DJ—a bit like James Bond, all suave and sophisticated.'

'Suave and sophisticated?' he repeated with a blink, never having thought of himself that way. 'I think I like that.'

'Not that I didn't like your old leather jacket *and* your snazzy motorbike leathers this morning,' she teased.

'Zo, tell me,' Zach said in a heavily faked Germanic accent. 'How long have you had zis leather fetish?'

Amy chuckled aloud, the serene grey of her eyes gleaming with her appreciation of his nonsense, and his spirits lifted still further.

'If I'd known you were coming to this thing, too, perhaps we could have come together,' he suggested, deliberately stifling the logical voice in the back of his head that was telling him to walk away now, while he still could. 'That way I wouldn't have had to dread standing around all by myself in a room full of strangers.'

'You needed someone to hold your hand?' she teased, and for just a moment he was tempted to do just that. He'd done nothing more than accidentally brush against her when they'd been tending a patient today, and the contact had felt electric. Had it been some sort of fluke reaction, or merely static electricity? Or had the awareness that had caused his teenaged self to spend endless hours fantasising survived fifteen years intact?

'Amy, dear,' said a cultured voice behind them. 'Do introduce us to your friend.'

The hairs went up on the back of his neck. It had been fifteen years since he'd last heard that voice but he'd never forgotten it…probably never would.

'Father,' Amy said with a smile as they turned to face the older couple standing behind them, but he took petty delight in the fact that it was a far less carefree one than those she'd bestowed on him. 'Hello, Mother. I've always loved that colour on you.'

'Amy.' The well-preserved woman returned her daughter's hug with such a restrained gentility that it seemed to Zach as though she was more worried about their greeting creasing the burgundy fabric of her dress than embracing her only child. 'Darling, why aren't you wearing the dress I sent over for you?'

'I'm sorry, Mother, but I didn't see it until I was almost ready to leave the house. If I'd stopped to change at that point, it would have made me late,' Amy said with every appearance of regret, but somehow Zach knew it was faked. There was a definite subtext to this conversation that was probably far more interesting than what was actually being said. He would have to get Amy to explain it later.

'And are you going to introduce us to your friend?' her father prompted, his grey eyes steely as he looked Zach over, no doubt totting up to the nearest small coin how much his evening suit had cost.

'Of course! How rude of me!' she exclaimed. 'Zach, these are my parents, Fiona and William Bowes Clark. Mother, Father, this is Dr Zachary Bowman. He's just joined the A and E staff at the hospital. You probably won't remember, but we actually went to school together in our final year before medical school.'

Zach saw the moment when Amy's father put two and two

together and knew that the man definitely *did* recognise his name, his new title and position only deepening the scowl.

'*Dr* Bowman?' he echoed in a tone of blatant disbelief, his expression more suited to someone who had just trodden in something noxious. He immediately turned to his daughter, angling his body to effectively exclude Zach from the rest of their conversation. 'Amy, your mother has put your name down at our table, next to Jeremy Crossley.'

Zach had been aware of the fact that Amy was incensed by her father's rudeness towards him, but if he hadn't been watching her, he wouldn't have caught the flash of discomfort behind her rigid smile at his announcement of their arrangements for her. Even when he saw her chin come up a combative inch, he couldn't guess what she was going to do.

'Oh, what a pity!' she exclaimed brightly, clearly not meaning a word. 'I won't be able to join your table because I've promised to be Zach's dinner companion. Perhaps you can introduce me to Mr Cross another time.'

'Cross*ley*,' her mother corrected eagerly. 'Jeremy Crossley...you remember? I told you that he's recently bought out one of your father's biggest suppliers?'

'How nice for him,' Amy said blandly, and Zach was hard-pressed not to laugh aloud. Suddenly, he understood exactly what was going on. Her parents had decided that it was time to find her another 'suitable' husband but whether it was because they were growing impatient to spoil some grand-children or merely the dynastic need to see their name and hefty financial inheritance passed down to the next genera-tion, it certainly wasn't because Amy was willing. The only thing he knew for certain was that her father definitely didn't consider *him* as anything close to suitable.

Well, that was just too bad, and if Amy wanted his help to exert her independence from their meddling, who was he to look a gift horse in the mouth?

'Sweetheart, I think everyone's started going through to find their tables,' he pointed out as he slid a proprietorial arm around her slender waist. 'Should we make a move?'

He held his breath when he felt her freeze under his blatantly possessive gesture and wondered for a moment whether she would humiliate him by rejecting his touch in front of her parents.

For several breathless seconds her silvery grey eyes looked into his while myriad questions filled them, but then he saw the impish spark of devilment take over a split second before she took the half-step closer to press her slender frame against him.

'What a good idea. It'll give us time to introduce ourselves to our dinner companions before we start eating.' She turned back briefly to speak to her blatantly disapproving parents. 'Have a lovely meal. I hope it raises loads of money. And if I don't see you again before we leave, I'll call you at the weekend.'

Zach wasn't capable of doing anything more than nodding in the speechless couple's direction before he turned to join the crowd now making their way towards a sumptuous room full of tables gleaming with cutlery and candles.

For a start, he couldn't believe that Amy had been so quick to come up with an excuse not to join her parents' choice of suitable dinner companion...one that involved *him*. Then there was the fact that she'd barely batted an eyelid when he'd called her 'sweetheart', or when he'd wrapped an arm around her. Only the fact that her eyes had darkened in response had told him of the deeper effect of his gesture on her.

Now she was actually walking by his side with her fingers deliberately threaded through his as though they were an established couple.

'*Sweetheart?*' she whispered out of the side of her mouth, one eyebrow raised, but her eyes were gleaming with suppressed mirth.

'Would you have preferred "darling"?' he asked hoarsely, surprised that his voice was working at all. He still wasn't absolutely certain that this wasn't just another adolescent dream.

'I wouldn't have cared what you called me, as long as it got me out of sitting with another of Mother's "prospects",' she said grimly.

'Oh, I see! I'm nothing more than the lesser of the two evils!' he exclaimed, even as he tried to absorb the blow without showing the hurt on his face. He should have known better than to set himself up for another—

'No! That's *not* what I meant at all!' Amy exclaimed sharply, then glanced from one side to the other to realise that they had several interested onlookers listening in to their conversation. 'Oh, we can't talk here!' she said crossly, and tightened her hand around his as she started to tow him out of the mêlée towards the side of the room.

'Is there a problem?' asked a helpful waiter, when he realised they were heading the wrong way.

Amy made an exasperated sound that perfectly expressed Zach's own feelings and gave him an idea.

'Amy, does the charity make any extra money if we actually sit down and eat the meal?' he asked, and saw her forehead pleat as she pondered the unexpected question.

'Not a penny—unless you were intending buying a large

number of raffle tickets!' she confirmed with a dawning grin that told him she'd followed his train of thought. 'What d'ya say we blow this joint?' she demanded in a dreadful Humphrey Bogart impersonation then returned to her normal voice. 'How do you fancy piping hot fish and chips instead of lukewarm rubber chicken?'

'Is the Friary still open for business?' He'd spent many months working in the family-owned take-away establishment to earn the money to pay for his bike but hadn't had time since he'd been back to even find out whether it was still a going concern.

'Of course it is!' she exclaimed, already hurrying out towards Reception, her strides swift and sure in spite of the impossibly slender heels that brought the top of her head up to the level of his eyes and her lips temptingly, conveniently close. 'The town wouldn't be the same without Melvin and Sheila's special crispy batter.'

They paused just long enough to retrieve her wrap but it wasn't until they were standing on the front steps of the hotel with his keys in his hand that she came to a sudden halt.

'Oh, Lord! I forgot!' she wailed. 'I can't go like this!'

For a moment he was flooded with the echoes of the blind rage that had consumed him fifteen years ago. What on earth had made him think that she'd changed in the interim? He should have known she would rather sit down to a civilised meal in sumptuous surroundings with Jeremy Crosseyes. Once a princess…

'I'm just not dressed to go riding around on a motorbike,' she continued, oblivious to his excoriating thoughts. 'I'd have to hike the hem of my dress halfway up my thighs.'

He laughed aloud. *That* was what she was worrying about?

'No problem,' he promised as he dangled the keys in front of her, displaying the car manufacturer's logo. He forced himself to ignore the vivid images her words had initiated of her skirt hiked far further than halfway up her thighs and those thighs wrapped tightly around his hips, or he'd disgrace himself in public. 'I didn't use the bike this evening.'

'Afraid you'd arrive with your teeth full of flies?' she teased as she followed him down the shallow steps to the gleaming car parked just a few feet away. 'Wow! This is rather swish! How fast does she go?'

'She obeys the speed limit all the way to the fish and chip shop,' he said firmly as he held the door open for her.

'Spoilsport!' She laughed up into his face and he had to tighten his grip on the door or he would have given in to the urge to taste the sweet curve of those lips.

He forced himself to concentrate on the fact that she was spoiled enough to be willing to risk the safety of other road users just for the thrill of speed, and could feel the frown darkening his face by the time he joined her in the cushioned luxury of the car.

'Hey, I was only asking how fast she *could* go, not asking you to break the limit,' she pointed out as he put the key in the ignition and started the engine with a refined purr. 'We both see enough of what happens when people ignore the rules.'

He sighed and dropped his head, unaccountably angry that he couldn't find something unappealing enough about the woman to counter the irresistible attraction he felt for her. If he wasn't careful, he was in danger of having history repeating itself.

'Sorry. I was...' He shrugged, totally unable to put his scrambled thoughts into words.

'Trying to put up barriers between us?' she suggested sharply, and he discovered that her brain hadn't lost any of the edge that had forced him to strive ever harder to keep up when they'd first known each other. She'd certainly put her finger on his feelings.

'Not that I blame you, after my father's display of bad manners,' she added, much to his surprise. 'It was totally inexcusable for him to—'

'To try to protect his little princess from the nasty commoner?' he suggested, the memory of that long-ago confrontation hardly faded at all, despite the fact it had happened fifteen years ago.

He saw the flash of anger in her eyes in spite of the low level of light in the car.

'I'm far too old to need my father's protection,' she said through gritted teeth, 'and as for seeing you as a nasty commoner…'

He already knew the answer to that—it was one of his more vivid memories from that disastrous summer. Neither did he believe that her father was ready to let her live her own life yet.

Suddenly, he was tired of the way something that couldn't be changed was having such an effect on what was happening *now*. He'd actually been enjoying the way they seemed to be able to pick up each other's thoughts. It had reminded him of the way they'd worked together as study partners, the two of them almost unbeatable…not that he'd ever received any of the praise. Their teachers had automatically assumed that he was merely hanging on to her coattails to get through his exams.

Did they have too much history between them to ever be

able to form some sort of workable relationship? Perhaps sharing a meal in the front of his car would give them the answer.

'Cod, plaice, haddock or skate?' he listed in a sing-song voice, almost as he had when he'd worked at the Friary. 'And will that be standard or a large portion of chips?'

He breathed a silent sigh of relief when she chuckled.

'No, don't tell me,' he warned before she could say anything. 'You'll want plaice with a small portion of chips with salt but no vinegar.'

'You're guessing!' she exclaimed in disbelief. 'You can't possibly remember what I used to order fifteen years ago!'

He remembered far more than that, he admitted silently as he drew up in front of his old place of work and glanced across at her, sitting there in all her finery, right down to the way her skin had felt when he'd brushed against it and the sweetly vanilla scent of it.

'Next question—do you want to go in to eat, or get a takeaway?'

'We're slightly overdressed for it, aren't we?' she said in resignation as she gazed out at the brightly-lit interior, and he wondered if she was as startled as he was that it had changed so little. 'But it would have been nice to say hi to Melvin and Sheila.'

'So, come in with me while I place our order,' he invited as he released both their seat-belts. 'They won't be able to murder me in front of witnesses.'

'Murder you?' She laughed. 'Why would they want to do that?'

'Because this is the first time I've visited since the day I got my exam results and took off,' he admitted rather shamefacedly, remembering how patiently the older couple had put up with his craziness in those weeks after the school leavers' dance. 'Melvin will probably take his filleting knife to me.'

'That I'd like to see.' She laughed even harder, probably at the image of the wiry little man who'd barely come up to his shoulder fifteen years ago. It would be Sheila, nearly twice his size, who would be the greater danger.

'One cod, large chips, one plaice, small chips,' he called out over the sound of the bell activated by the opening of the door.

The busy clatter halted for several beats while two heads swivelled sharply in the direction of his voice.

'Zach!' shrieked Sheila, instantly abandoning her post behind the till to hurry towards him, her arms already extended in her desire to snatch him into a hug.

'Damn, boy, what took you so long?' Melvin roared, unable to leave the bubbling tank that seethed with rapidly browning chipped potatoes.

'Look at you! All dressed up like the dog's dinner!' Sheila exclaimed as she came to a screeching halt in front of him, clearly too intimidated to touch him.

'Never could do a thing to please you,' he complained as he wrapped both arms around her, a potential dry-cleaning bill nothing in comparison to this sort of welcome. He was startled for a moment by how much weight she'd lost since he'd last seen her. Had she finally taken government warnings about obesity seriously? 'When I worked here, you were always on at me to smarten up a bit.'

'You never listened to me before,' she pointed out as she stepped back and swatted at him as if he were an annoying fly. 'Anyway, where are the two of you off to dressed up to the nines? Some slap-up do?'

'No. We just thought we'd like some fish and chips for supper,' he said blandly.

Sheila peered a little closer at his companion and he held his breath, waiting in trepidation and suddenly wondering if he'd made an embarrassing mistake. He saw the moment when recognition dawned.

'Well, well!' she marvelled. 'Look at that, Melvin. Our Zach finally got to take his princess out and he can't think of anywhere better to take her than here.'

Zech felt the colour rise in his cheeks and from the twinkle in Amy's eyes he knew she'd seen it.

'Actually, we were at that big do to raise money for the hospital,' she explained. 'But when we realised that we had a choice between trying to eat a plate of rubber chicken or coming here…' She shrugged. 'Well, here we are.'

'So, where do you want to eat this fish?' demanded Melvin as he hoisted the basked of golden-brown food out of the fryer to allow it to drain. 'Here or take-away?'

Zach was just about to tell him to put their meal on two plates, suddenly looking forward to spending time with the couple who had cared more about him than any blood relative, when the bell jangled furiously, announcing the arrival of a boisterous group of teenage boys.

'Whooee!' said one of the boys as he saw the way Zach was dressed then took his time eyeing Amy up and down. 'This place is coming up in the world.'

For a moment, when he saw the way the scruffy youth was ogling every one of Amy's slender inches, Zach was tempted to deck him. It was totally irrelevant that *he'd* been staring lasciviously at them all evening.

Amy was obviously totally unperturbed. 'This place has

been the best in the town for at least thirty years,' she said firmly, then smiled her thanks as Melvin held aloft the small carrier bag containing their meals, having made the decision for them.

Zach stepped forward, one hand automatically reaching into his pocket for his wallet until Melvin glared at him, silently telling him to leave it where it was.

'Don't be a stranger,' the older man ordered, only releasing his hold on the bag when Zach nodded, then glanced across at Amy. 'And that goes for you, too, missy,' he added gruffly. 'This place could do with a bit of glamour now and again, so don't wait for this great lump to bring you.'

Amy agreed with a smile but even though she hastily turned away, it wasn't soon enough to hide the suspicious brightness in her eyes. His own had a suspicious prickle to them, especially when she'd been greeted with every bit as much welcome as he had.

Well, there went his reputation as the hard case of the chemistry class. She'd never believe his stone-faced persona now that she'd seen—

'Hey, babe,' began one of the youngsters, cocky in his teenage self-belief. 'How about ditching him and joining us for a bit of—' Zach turned and silently fixed him with a killer glare and the youth's jaunty invitation died away to silence.

'How do you *do* that?' Amy demanded a couple of minutes later before he even had a chance to settle himself in his seat beside her.

'Do what?' He turned to face her and when he saw the way the light outlined her perfect features he barely stopped himself groaning aloud, especially when his pulse was still pounding from the sudden surge of testosterone caused by...

'That cold glare,' she said, interrupting his hormone-laden thoughts. 'You used to do it at school, too, and it still stops anyone in their tracks. It even used to work on the teachers… in fact, it *especially* used to work on the teachers,' she continued in a musing voice. 'I think it used to frighten them.'

'Were you frightened, too?' His hand froze on the ignition key. The thought was like a kick to his gut.

'No!' She chuckled, a sweet ripple of sound that almost instantly released the tension holding every muscle rigid. 'It reminded me of a dog my grandmother took in. He wasn't much more than a puppy but from the number of scars on its body you could tell he'd been badly treated.'

Zach didn't know whether being compared to a stray mutt was any better for his ego than thinking she'd been afraid of him.

'Anyway,' she continued, apparently oblivious to the damage she was doing to his pride, 'even when he was full grown and knew we would never hurt him, he never lost that reflex. All it took was for someone to raise their hand or even raise their voice near my grandmother and me and all his hackles would go up, his lip would curl to show his teeth and he'd get *that* look in his eyes.'

'Remind me not to growl,' he said shortly as he put the car into gear, shaken that she'd pegged him quite so accurately. That was exactly the way he'd been feeling when that punk had started trying to chat Amy up…protective…possessive…and definitely ready to rip his throat out!

No change there, then, he admitted on a sigh as he turned away from town, automatically heading towards the long straight stretch of road that had beckoned to him whenever everything got on top of him that year.

'Are we going to Beacon Hill?'

It wasn't until she asked that he realised that was exactly where he was heading.

'If you don't mind? I didn't even think…'

'I don't mind at all. It's one of my favourite places when I want to do some thinking. There's something about the atmosphere up there that just seems to help put everything in perspective…'

'Perhaps it's got something to do with all those centuries of history,' he suggested, shaken anew that she should feel the same way about the place. 'I remember the first time I heard about the chain of beacons right around the country and the way they would be lit to warn of invasion.'

'Me, too!' she exclaimed. 'I was fascinated by the idea that they were spaced just far enough apart on hills so that they were visible in the distance from each other, and that as soon as one was burning, the next one along lit theirs and so on. With our background of modern cars and telephones it seemed impossible that such an ancient method of communication could happen many times faster than a rider on the fastest horse could possibly have delivered the message…'

'At least, these days, they're used for more ceremonial duties like celebrating the Queen's Jubilee or the two-hundredth anniversary of Trafalgar,' he added as he drew up beside the ancient stone platform.

Darkness descended as soon as he switched off the lights, not wanting to drain the battery once the engine was silent, and with that silence came a sudden feeling of intimacy that made his pulse take up a heavier rhythm.

How many times had he thought about just this situation…the two of them up here in the night…alone…?

'It's almost as if we're the last two people left on earth,' Amy whispered, obviously feeling the same sense of awe that the sight always brought to him. 'There's just us and the stars and the wind.'

'*And* all the lights spread out down there,' he pointed out deliberately, needing to do something to bring his thoughts back to earth or he'd be tempted to drag her into his arms the way he'd longed to all those years ago. 'There must be nearly as many of them as there are stars, more's the pity.'

'You mean, because of the light pollution?' Amy asked. 'Does it really make that much difference? After all, we do need to be able to see where we're going, for safety's sake.'

'If you'd ever seen a sky filled with a billion stars stretching from horizon to horizon, every one of them clear and bright and all of them seeming close enough to touch…well, I certainly think it's worthwhile taking an extra couple of seconds looking both ways before I cross a road if it would help to get rid of some of those streetlights,' he said, then realised just how fervent he sounded. She'd be thinking that he had some weird bee in his bonnet about way-out environmental—

'You've seen it?' she interrupted, almost eagerly, apparently unaware of anything other than what they were talking about. 'You've seen a sky like that? Where? When?'

'Africa. At first, right on the border of South Africa, to be precise, when I volunteered for a short stint in one of the refugee camps with one of the emergency relief organisations.' Only half of his mind was on what he was saying, the rest fully occupied with the fact that he actually had ABC in his car and that she was close enough for him to smell the vanilla-and-spice fragrance of her perfume and see the way her eyes widened as she drank in what he was saying. It was heady stuff. Every bit as heady as his imagination had painted it.

'Africa! That's right!' she exclaimed with a smile that almost seemed to light up the shadows of the car. 'But someone said you'd been in one of the big hospitals out there, getting a bit of experience under your belt.'

'I did that, too, after my stint as a volunteer was over.'

'What was it like?' she was obviously eager for details.

'Scary,' he admitted bluntly. 'When you're fairly newly qualified, there are just so many situations that you've only heard about…like someone coming in with multiple gunshot wounds who's closely followed by half a dozen others who've been gunned down in reprisal for the first one's injuries…and you've never even dealt with *one* GSW before and now you're having to do it with only half the monitoring equipment you need. On the other hand, because it was a hospital in the rough end of the city, the staff was well accustomed to that sort of thing and they were able to baby me through the first one.'

'Definitely scary,' she said with a shudder. 'I thought it was bad enough when I was the most senior member of staff available one night when we had a multiple RTA, a heart attack and a precipitate prem birth all arrive at once.'

'And you're instantly convinced that you can't remember a single thing and every one of them is going to die and it'll all be your fault,' he suggested, and felt an answering grin spread across his face when she burst out laughing.

The laughter was cut short by a muted sound that had Amy scrabbling inside her bag for her mobile phone.

He saw her expression change when she caught sight of the number displayed on the screen.

'Damn,' she muttered, and pulled a distinctly unladylike face as she pressed the button to answer the call.

The conversation was just cryptic enough for him to know that she was speaking to another man, but the surge of jealousy hardly had time to gather before he realised just which man had invaded the private cocoon that had surrounded the two of them since they'd left the fundraiser.

'No, Father,' she said on a sigh, and he was assailed by an emotion very different from jealousy—something far darker. 'I've already left the hotel.'

Zach couldn't hear what the man was saying but he could imagine.

'No, Father, I'm not coming all the way back just to meet one of your business colleagues. There's no point in—'

'I said *no*, Father,' she repeated quietly but firmly, using the same tone he'd heard when she was dealing with one of their more difficult patients. 'I'll speak to you soon.'

Zach could just imagine how *that* was going down with her over-protective father, especially knowing that she was in *his* company.

'No. *Not* tonight,' she said decisively, clearly intending to end the conversation any moment. 'It'll be far too late to ring you by the time I get home. Enjoy the rest of your evening.'

As he watched, she deliberately pressed the button to end the call, cutting her father off in mid-splutter, then, equally deliberately, pressed the button to turn the phone off completely before dropping it into her bag and closing it.

Only then did she cover her face with both hands. 'How embarrassing!' she muttered, then gave vent to a sound that was a weird combination of a shriek and a groan.

CHAPTER FOUR

'SOMETIMES, I could almost hate my father,' Amy muttered under her breath for the umpteenth time that week as she watched Zach disappearing around the corner.

After all those months of sitting starry-eyed next to him in a classroom, and all those years of 'what if' fantasies, she'd finally been sitting in Zach's car on a starlit night…and her father had phoned her.

'Checking up on me as if I were still a schoolgirl, for heaven's sake!' she growled between clenched teeth as she signed off on the treatment she'd given her latest patient, pausing in her litany of complaints just long enough to check that the quantities of drugs she'd given for pain relief had been recorded accurately. She'd never be able to forgive herself if someone was given an accidental overdose on the strength of her own poor record-keeping.

'Problem, Amy, girl?' queried a voice at her elbow, and she looked up into Louella's frowning face.

'No…well, nothing more than the usual…my father sticking his nose in where it isn't wanted,' Amy grumbled, knowing that Louella wouldn't rest until she ferreted out whatever was worrying her; she just couldn't help her nurturing side coming out, even in a busy department.

Louella snorted, having heard the same complaint several times since Amy had started working in A and E. 'There are some that don't seem to understand that people can't be treated the same as figures on a balance sheet, moved about from one column to another to make the answer you want. Can't you get your mother to stop him interfering?'

'Some hope!' Amy scoffed. 'She'll be standing on the sidelines, cheering him on. She'd like nothing better than to see me waltzing up the aisle again, on the way to producing a clutch of picture-perfect grandchildren for her to boast about to her fellow committee members.'

'And you don't want that?' Louella probed gently as she led Amy towards the staff lounge and a reviving drink. 'Is it that you don't want children at all, or is it still too soon to think about marrying again? You don't mind my asking, do you?' she added hastily. 'Just tell me to mind my own business if I'm opening the wounds, only…well, you never speak about your husband, so no one quite dares to mention…'

'It's not that I don't want children,' Amy admitted in a rush, suddenly needing to speak honestly about her tangled feelings, the way she never could with her mother. Usually, the two of them worked opposite shifts, with Louella preferring to work while her children were asleep, but for the next week she'd done a swap with another member of staff, and Amy was just learning the delights of having a confidante. 'If it had been just my decision, we'd have started a family almost straight away, but Edward …' She paused, suddenly realising that to say any more would be disloyal to her husband. His reasons for delaying their first child—waiting until they'd both got their professional lives running smooth-ly—had seemed perfectly rational at the time.

She sighed. 'It's just that the two of them keep arranging blind dates for me, and it's getting more and more embarrass-ing. I hate it because I have absolutely nothing in common with their candidates, most of whom are connected to my father's business in some way, and we have nothing to say to each other. It's especially awkward with my parents sitting there listening to every word we say, as though they expect an engagement to be announced within the first half-hour.'

'Grim! So, what are these men like, girl?' Louella de-manded with a chuckle as she handed over a steaming mug and settled herself into the opposite corner of the slightly shabby settee. 'Are they wealthy? Good-looking? Sexy? All of the above?'

'I presume they're all relatively wealthy, otherwise my father wouldn't look at them as possible sons-in-law, but as for good-looking or sexy...that hardly matters if they can't hold a conversation about anything other than money. I'm hard-pressed not to yawn in their faces halfway through the meal.'

'Oops! Definitely not good for the male ego!' Louella laughed aloud this time. 'So what are you going to do about it?'

'There's not a lot I *can* do,' Amy said glumly. 'I manage to duck as many "command performances" as I can—work-ing on A and E helps there, because I can always fudge the number of hours I spend on duty to avoid them. But as I can't cut my parents out of my life completely, they still manage to ambush me as I arrive at each 'do' and tell me that they've arranged for me to sit beside their next candidate...' As they had the other evening when Zach had come to her rescue.

'Well, how about practising a bit of preventative medicine, then?' Louella suggested. 'You'll have to take your own man along each time, so they can't do it to you.'

'That's all very well in theory, but as I haven't got any suitable candidates lined up…'

'Amy, girl, I don't believe that for a moment. You're beautiful and far too slim for a woman of my size to be happy standing beside you, you're intelligent and you've got a good job. If you weren't sending out keep-off vibes, you could have them standing in line, wanting to take you out. What about starting with Zach?' Louella proposed with a wicked grin. 'Tall, dark and handsome—he'd be perfect!'

'Perfect for what?' Zach demanded suspiciously as he came within earshot at just the wrong moment. He completely buried Amy's muttered, 'Chance would be a fine thing!'

'The perfect candidate for Amy, girl to fend off—'

'Louella! Don't!' Amy interrupted hastily, only too aware that there were far too many pairs of ears all around them and mortified that Zach might feel obliged to take her out as a charity case. He'd already made his preference very clear by avoiding her ever since that night. It would only make everything so much more embarrassing if Louella were to speak to him about it.

And why had she expected anything else? she thought, cross with herself that she obviously hadn't grown out of that teenage crush, even after all this time.

Nevertheless, there was a definite irony in the fact that the situation hadn't changed for either of them, she thought as she rinsed out her coffee-mug and made her way to the door. She was still hopelessly longing for him to discover that she was the love of his life, and he was still totally disinterested.

'Dr Willmott! What a lovely surprise!' exclaimed a hearty voice almost as soon as she emerged into the reception area, and even as she turned to face the florid man bearing down on her she could feel her heart sinking. 'Fancy seeing *you* here, my dear,' he gushed.

'Mr Spruitt-West,' she said, hoping her smile looked a little more genuine than it felt, especially as the man was surrounded by a coterie of the hospital's administrative bigwigs.

'Geoffrey, my dear. Do call me Geoffrey,' he invited, sidling far too close to her for her peace of mind. She cringed when she saw the expression in his protruding pale eyes and the way he licked his lips as he examined her from head to foot. 'I was just saying how sad we were that you left us, but we understood that there would have been far too many memories of dear Edward for you to stay.'

And it hadn't *just* been the memories she'd been hoping to leave behind, she thought darkly, remembering all too clearly that 'dear Geoffrey' hadn't been the only one of her former colleagues to assume that a relatively young widow might be feeling lonely and wanting a little comforting.

'You've settled in well, I hope?' He gave a cursory glance around the department but Amy doubted that he'd actually focussed on anything. He had a different agenda and she had a sinking feeling that she knew exactly what it was.

'Very well, thank you,' she said with a smile that included his similarly grey-suited companions, wondering idly whether grey suits were part of a uniform you were expected to adopt once you reached a certain level of the hospital hierarchy. Edward had worn something very similar even before his appointment had been confirmed…

Another picture leapt into her head and she had to suppress a grin at the thought that she couldn't imagine Zach ever conforming quite so eagerly. She wouldn't be the least bit surprised, when the time came, if he was the only consultant arriving on a motorbike, sporting head-to-toe leather.

'I've travelled up here to present a paper tomorrow evening, but I've got a free evening tonight,' her former colleague bulldozed on, finally coming to the point of this 'accidental' meeting. 'If you let me have your new address, I could call for you to take you out for a meal. Would seven o'clock leave you enough time to change after you finish work?'

Seven millennia wouldn't be enough time for her to want to go out with this louse. Apart from the fact that the thought of spending any time with him made her skin crawl, he was a married man. Didn't it matter to him that Amy not only knew that he had a wife but had met the poor woman at nearly every social occasion the hospital had put on for the last five years?

'I'm *so* sorry, Mr Spruitt-West, but I already have plans for this evening,' she said coolly, glad that she didn't have to tell him that even putting a load of laundry through the machine was infinitely more attractive than spending a single second in his presence.

His bloated face darkened with anger that she was daring to turn him down yet again, and in front of so many witnesses. Was that why he'd made the invitation here, believing that she would meekly agree rather than cause any unpleasantness?

'Oh, but surely—' began one of the more obsequious administrators, but Amy wasn't about to let a mere paper-pusher interfere in her life.

'I'm sorry, gentlemen,' she interrupted hastily, taking

several steps away from the group so that she was almost talking over her shoulder to them. 'As you know, we're *severely* understaffed in the department and if we're to have *any* hope of keeping to the government's performance targets, I really must get back to work. We wouldn't like the hospital to have to pay thousands of pounds in penalty fines—that would just make the problems worse, wouldn't it?' And she spun on one heel and made for the closest treatment room, regardless of the fact that she had no idea if there was even a patient in there.

She shouldered her way briskly thought one of the doors and nearly cannoned into Zach just inside the room.

'Sorry,' she said through gritted teeth, then drew in a deep breath and blew it out slowly and deliberately, grateful for some strange reason that he was the only person to see the way she'd lost her cool. At least she'd held it together when she'd been face to face with that loathsome toad.

'Really?' he asked, and for the first time in over a week she saw a gleam in those dark eyes. 'How sorry?'

'What? Well, I'm definitely sorry that it wasn't *him* that I nearly flattened with the door,' she muttered darkly. 'Obnoxious, slimy…'

'But what about *me*?' Zach demanded. 'What about *my* narrow escape? What about *my* hurt feelings? What about my fear that I was about to be permanently injured by your thoughtless actions?'

Amy took one glance at his pathetic attempt at looking… well, pathetic, and she couldn't stop the smile lifting the corners of her mouth. If there was anyone *less* pathetic than this prime specimen of manhood…

'Thank you,' she said, surprised that he'd managed to lift her mood so easily.

'For what?' Now he was making an equally pathetic attempt at looking innocent.

She sent him an old-fashioned look and he dropped the pretence. 'I couldn't help hearing your parting shot,' he admitted, and shook his head. 'You were always quick-witted, ABC, but you've obviously been honing the edge of your tongue. It's sharp enough to clip a hedge.'

The picture his words conjured up inside her head made her laugh out loud.

'One of my more private accomplishments,' she agreed, playing along with his foolishness.

'So, will it be gratitude or guilt?' he demanded obliquely, when the laughter faded and the ensuing silence stretched just a little too long between them.

'Will *what* be…?' She shook her head. 'You've lost me, I'm afraid.'

Under his breath he muttered something about working hard, but it was said too softly for her to hear, and before she could ask him to repeat it, he was speaking aloud again. 'Will it be gratitude for lifting your spirits, or guilt for nearly putting me in ICU that makes you agree to come out with me?'

Amy felt her eyes widen with disbelief and her pulse definitely stuttered for several beats before starting again at twice its normal rate. Strange how very different her reaction was to two similar invitations in the space of a few minutes, she thought, even as she shook her head.

'Neither,' she said, fighting to keep a victory grin off her face. After avoiding her for so long, he'd cracked before she had, but it had been a close-run thing. She'd actually been starting to think she was going to have to make the first move to build a comfortable working relationship with the stubborn man.

His face fell, and this time she knew that it wasn't a feigned expression because it took him several telling seconds to bring it under control.

'Neither gratitude nor guilt would persuade me to go out with you, but…' She paused significantly, wondering if she dared to continue, wondering if he would think she had completely taken leave of her senses.

'But…?' he repeated warily, one dark eyebrow raised in exactly the same way he used to face down his teachers so long ago.

'But…' She tilted her chin up and deliberately met those dark, all-seeing eyes. 'I might be persuaded if you promised to take me for a ride on your bike.'

Yes! she exulted when she saw the shock he hadn't been able to hide.

'You want me to…? You want to…?'

Incoherence? She didn't think she'd ever heard him at a loss for words, especially when he'd been her teenage idol.

'Well? Yes or no?' she challenged urgently, spurred on by noises in the corridor outside the room and all too aware that they were unlikely to have it to themselves for much longer. The department was far too busy for rooms to remain idle for any length of time.

'When?' he demanded bluntly, his own eyes flicking swiftly towards the doors, telling her he was equally aware of their limited time.

'Tonight?' She would certainly rather be out on the back

of Zach's noisy beast than waiting for her underwear to finish spinning. 'As soon as we finish work?'

The decision was made with barely a pause. 'You're on…on two conditions.'

'Two?'

'First, that you'll let me provide you with the right safety gear…helmet and so on.'

'Agreed. And second?'

'That you'll tell me what had you in such a temper that you nearly assaulted me with that door.'

'Assaulted!' she spluttered, but didn't have time to say any more as the door in question was thrust urgently towards them, closely followed by a swiftly moving trolley.

Zach grabbed her arm to pull her out of harm's way and held on even when she would have moved away, pulling her back against the lean strength of his body so that she was aware of him with every molecule.

'Yes or no?' he demanded softly, his breath warm against the side of her neck. 'And bear in mind that this is a deal-breaker. No conversation, no ride.'

How did he know that she'd intended trying to slide out of that part of the bargain? The last thing she wanted to do when she was finally living one of her fondest fantasies was to have to talk about her slimy former colleague.

'Deal?' he prompted, obviously wanting to have the matter settled before he released her, and with the panting para-medic trying to maintain chest compressions on the patient while it was pushed towards them, that meant immediately.

'Deal,' she agreed, her reluctance warring with the excite-ment that suddenly surged through her as she left him to his task, unsurprised to see that he'd switched instantaneously into the consummate professional, his mind totally focused on the shattered body in front of him as he listened to the paramedic giving his report on their patient's injuries.

Amy vaguely worried that she would find it hard to keep her mind on her own work with this evening's outing in prospect, but within seconds of their bargain, before she'd even reached the dreaded board or checked on the lab results she'd ordered, she was being waylaid in the corridor and all her instincts switched into doctor mode.

'Are you a doctor?' pleaded a young woman with a small child in her arms. 'Please, tell me you're a doctor!'

For just a moment Amy was tempted to brush her off and to insist that the young woman should take the sleeping child back to wait her turn—there was a reason why triage was performed—but there was something about the child's awkward position in her mother's arms and the expression of panic in the widely dilated eyes that made her stop.

'Yes. I'm Dr Willmott. Has someone seen you?'

'Please, I won't take up much of your time…just a moment or two…' she interrupted hurriedly. 'It's just so I can be sure…' The child in her arms gave a fretful whimper and the strangely high-pitched sound of it sent a little shiver up the back of Amy's neck.

'This is my daughter, Amelie, and I'm Lorraine,' she began hurriedly. 'She wasn't well when she woke up this morning so I phoned our GP to ask him to visit, but the receptionist said he wouldn't waste his time coming out for a child with a cold and insisted I take her to the practice.' She gasped for breath, her words getting faster and faster and her voice getting higher, her fear clearly growing with her story.

Amy's instincts were telling her that it was worth listening. It was time to get the child out of the corridor and start doing a proper examination so she started to guide the mother into the nearest vacant treatment room without interrupting her.

'Then,' she continued, 'when I got there, the receptionist said he'd been called out to someone else and she said they didn't know how long he'd be, and they wanted me to make an appointment for tomorrow afternoon, but I don't think she can wait that long,' she ended, almost in tears.

'So, what do *you* think is the matter with her?' Amy asked as she peered into the tiny face nestled against her mother's shoulder, her fingers registering the ominous heat radiating off her blotchy skin but the tiny starfish hands felt cold in spite of the fact that the child was feverish.

'*Me? What do I think?*' The woman seemed stunned that Amy would even ask, giving up her precious burden without a murmur to let Amy lay her on the trolley and begin stripping her clothing away.

'Well, you *are* her mother and you know her better than anyone else in the world,' Amy said with a swift glance up into the young mother's pale face and an encouraging smile. 'You knew that there was something wrong with her when she woke up this morning. So, tell me what you noticed.'

'She's only five months old and usually she loves her food, but this morning she refused to have anything, and she's got diarrhoea and she's miserable and cries every time I have to change her nappy, and she didn't even want to have a cuddle and…'

She ran out of breath but Amy didn't really need to hear any more. She could see for herself that the child on the trolley in front of her was lying with her back unnaturally arched and her neck retracted and that, in spite of the feverish temperature of her body, her skin was pale and blotchy.

'Is it meningitis?'

The words were whispered with dread, but they might as well have been shouted. 'I know she hasn't got that special rash, but I've got this little card—I picked it up off the counter at the chemist just after Amelie was born—and it shows you what to look for.' She took one of the familiar little cards produced by the Meningitis Trust out of her pocket to show it to Amy.

'There *is* a possibility,' Amy admitted. 'And it's brilliant that you didn't wait until tomorrow for an appointment because now we can do some tests straight away. That way, hopefully we can set your mind at rest, but either way we can start treating Amelie immediately *in case* it's meningitis.'

Zach appeared as if by magic just when she was preparing to perform the lumbar puncture that would provide the sample of spinal fluid that would give them the definitive diagnosis. She drew a steadying breath while she checked that she had all the kit she needed, including a disposable spinal needle, manometer and three-way tap with three numbered sterile bottles and a fluoride bottle for the blood glucose sample to be taken before the puncture.

'Have you done an LP on one so small?' Zach asked quietly when she'd finished injecting the analgesic to numb the area, pitching his words low enough so they were covered by the activity in the busy department around them.

Amy shook her head, meeting the dark watchful eyes above his mask to admit candidly, 'And I'd really rather not take the time to practise on her when she might not have time to spare.'

Zach gave a single nod and without any fanfare reversed positions with her so that she was the one holding the child in position when the time came for the all-important needle to be introduced between the tiny vertebrae.

His technique was swift and flawless and in no time the vital samples were on their way to the lab.

'Phone Paeds and tell them she's coming up,' Zach said over his shoulder.

'I've already spoken to them,' Amy said. 'Until we've got a diagnosis she can't go on a ward in case it's contagious, and they haven't got a single room free. She'll have to go in one of the isolation rooms off the observation ward.'

The young mother gave a keening cry, clearly following every word of their conversation. 'Does that mean she's dying?'

'Not at all, Lorraine,' Amy said, hurrying to wrap a comforting arm around the young woman who had stoically sat reassuring her little daughter throughout the procedure, even though every instinct must have been rebelling against having a needle stuck into her child's spine. 'It's just a precaution until we know exactly what we're dealing with.'

'There are several forms of meningitis, some more contagious than others,' Zach explained gently even as he was preparing the child for transport up to the observation ward at the other end of the department. 'We don't even know whether it *is* meningitis, yet, but just in case it is, we don't want to risk anyone else catching it. Has she been in contact with many people in the last few days? Does she go to a crèche?'

'No. I'm the only one, apart from a couple of minutes at the doctor's surgery this morning. My partner's away, working.'

'And your family?' Amy prompted. 'When did they last see Amelie?'

'They haven't,' she said quietly, her shoulders slumping still further. 'They didn't approve of Didier, and when I fell pregnant…' She shook her head.

Amy's hackles rose on the young woman's behalf, and she felt an instant kinship as she silently railed at the arrogance of parents who thought they had the right to dictate who their children should fall in love with. Still, this situation was slightly different. There was a child to consider. A grandchild who, if things went badly, could even die before her grandparents saw her.

None of your business, she lectured herself sternly as she checked that the case notes were complete before they set off, ready to hand over to the observation ward staff, but she couldn't help noticing that Lorraine had given her parents' contact details on the initial form, neither could she stop the silent plotting that began. Things would move very quickly now, with powerful antibiotics already dripping into Amelie's system. Within half an hour or so the little one would be installed in an isolation room and the long, terrifying wait would begin.

'Thank you,' Lorraine said suddenly, pausing in her headlong rush to follow her daughter to grab Amy's arm. 'Thank you for listening to me, even though…'

'You're welcome, sweetheart,' Amy said and gave her a swift hug. 'Now, don't let them get away from you or you might not find your daughter again for years. This hospital can be a confusing maze unless you know your way around.'

The young woman gave a watery chuckle and sped off after her precious child.

Zach's 'Well spotted!' later in the day gave her a warm glow of satisfaction that nearly offset the guilt she felt after her meddling phone call.

She really had tried to reason herself out of doing it, but the thought that Lorraine was faced with going through something so frightening all by herself had tipped the balance between restraint and interfering.

Lorraine's mother had sounded so similar to her own that she'd almost apologised and put the phone down before she'd started, but the memory of that helpless little baby up in isolation had stiffened her resolve and she'd introduced herself briskly.

'Mrs Tennant? This is Dr Willmott and I work in Accident and Emergency in—'

'Accident and Emergency?' the woman interrupted sharply. 'Has something happened to my husband?'

'No, it's not your husband. It's your daughter. She came in this morning with her—'

'In that case, it's nothing to do with me,' she cut in brusquely, her voice cold now, rather than concerned. 'She made her choice and she's got to live with it.'

'So, you don't care that your granddaughter might be dying of meningitis?' Amy snapped back, incensed by her callousness. 'In that case, I apologise for bothering you.'

'Meningitis!' The word emerged from the phone halfway between a gasp and a shriek just as Amy was about to put the handset down. 'She's not…? She isn't…? How sick is she?' she managed after several false starts.

'We won't know for several hours—until we get the results of the tests,' Amy admitted. 'But if it *is* meningitis…well…' She really didn't want to list the full range of complications that could afflict such a young baby but, on the other hand, if it helped her make a decision about supporting her daughter…

She crossed her fingers and began again. 'Mrs Tennant, you probably know from news reports that in cases of septicaemia some children have had to have their arms and legs amputated to save their lives, and some are left with severe brain damage, so if you wanted a chance to see her while she's…' Amy deliberately let her voice die away, but when she heard a suppressed sob in the silence on the other end of the phone, she felt the dreadful weight of guilt descend on her again.

'And my daughter,' Mrs Tennant asked tentatively, almost choking on the words. 'How is she…coping?'

'She's an amazing young woman and you should be proud of her,' Amy responded bluntly, throwing caution to the wind. 'But at the moment, especially while she's waiting to find out what's wrong with Amelie, I know she really needs her mother's love to support her.'

CHAPTER FIVE

AMY was running more than half an hour late when she reached the end of her shift.

'When have I *ever* been able to leave on time?' she demanded of her steamy bathroom as she rubbed shampoo into her hair as part of the end-of-shift shower routine she'd started early on in her training, when she'd realised just how easy it would be to carry any infection home with her. It also meant that she could lose the hospital smell from her hair and skin before Zach arrived, and while she could try to fool herself that this evening's outing was nothing more than an attempt at forging a relaxed working atmosphere between the two of them, if she was honest…

Well, if she *was* honest, she would have to admit that having Zach see her as a friendly colleague was a long way down her list, and if the subtle spicy-vanilla perfume of her soap and the dabs of matching essence she dotted behind her ears and in her cleavage helped him to see her as a desirable woman…

Whoa!

She hauled her thoughts to a screeching halt and examined them.

Was that what she was doing? Was that what she really wanted?

It was all very well deciding to fulfil a teenage fantasy to ride on the back of his motorbike, but surely, that was *all* it was. It was far too soon after losing Edward for her to even *think* about… She wasn't ready to…

'Ha! Tell that to my hormones!' she muttered, her face heating with the realisation that her mind might not be ready but her body was another matter. In fact, where Zach was concerned…

'Enough!' she scolded herself, dragging a wide-toothed comb through her tangled hair. 'You'd better get moving or you're going to be greeting him at the door in your birthday suit, all pink and steaming from the shower.'

As it was, she'd barely managed to zip up a pair of fine black wool trousers and pull a cranberry-coloured jumper over the top when the doorbell rang, catching her barefoot and with her hair still damply draped over her shoulders.

She released the catch with fingers that shook visibly with excitement and there he was.

'Zach! Come in,' she invited breathlessly, her eyes busily taking in the fact that, in head-to-toe leather, he could have walked straight out of one of her favourite fantasies.

As he stepped into her well-lit hallway his pupils should have constricted, but as his eyes went over her, taking in the evidence that she'd recently emerged from the shower, she saw them dilate darkly.

Her heart gave a hopeful leap that it was proof that he was just as affected by looking her over as she was by the sight of him in his 'bad boy' leathers.

'You haven't changed much,' she blurted, but it wasn't

quite true. He still looked every bit as lean and athletic, but his shoulders were wider now, and his thighs more heavily muscled. And she was supposed to plaster herself against *that* when she climbed on the bike behind him? 'Um, is that the same jacket you used to wear to school?' she asked feebly, half-afraid that she was going to hyperventilate in front of him if she didn't get hold of her thoughts.

'No.' He grinned wryly, as though remembering the battles he'd had with their old headmaster who'd tried to ban him from wearing it, but was there a huskier edge than usual to his voice? *'This* is my old one…' He swung forward an infinitely scruffier leather jacket that he'd been holding over his shoulder by the chain at the back of the neck and held it out towards her, suspended from one lean finger. 'You're going to need it if you're not going to freeze.' She took it from him and looked down at it, tentatively touching the scuffed surface and remembering all the times she'd wished she'd felt free to stroke this supple leather, preferably with Zach inside it.

'You'll also need to change into some jeans, if you've got any,' he suggested. 'The fabric's thicker and more protective than those.' He gestured towards her smart trousers quite dismissively and she felt a pang of pique that she'd actually spent time choosing something flattering to wear.

'I won't be a minute,' she said tartly, and strode swiftly back into her bedroom, determined that this time she was going to ignore the way her outfit looked as long as it would keep her warm under the jacket he'd lent her.

Two minutes later she had donned a thick jumper and was zipping herself into an ancient pair of jeans—old favourites that she'd considered and discarded originally because they were the most disreputable thing she owned. A quick glance in her mirror confirmed that they were far more figure-hugging than her mother would ever have approved of, but when she shrugged her way into the leather jacket…

The doorbell rang again as she came out of her bedroom and she was still retrieving her damp hair from the neck of the jacket as she released the catch.

'Mr Pruitt-West!' she said, stunned to see him standing on her doorstep with a wide, self-satisfied smile on his face. 'What…? How…?' She was almost speechless. He was the very *last* person she'd wanted to see.

'My dear!' He stepped forward as though to embrace her in the continental way and she stepped hastily back. Unfortunately, that gave him the opportunity to invade her hallway just far enough to prevent her shutting the door.

'What are you doing here?' she demanded sharply, shuddering with distaste at the avid expression that spread over his face when he took in what she was wearing. 'How did you get my address?' If someone at the hospital had given it out, there would be hell to pay.

It was almost as if he knew exactly what she was thinking.

'I asked the hospital director if he could give me your parents' phone number,' he explained with oily self-assurance, knowing she could hardly object to that.

Unfortunately, Amy knew exactly how that call would have gone as if she'd eavesdropped. As soon as he mentioned who he was and that he was trying to get in touch with Amy, her mother would have fallen all over herself to give him her address. The only surprise was that she hadn't provided a personal escort.

'So, now that I'm here,' he continued confidently, his eyes still crawling all over the tight fit of her jeans, 'do you want to change into something a little more up-market so I can take you out for a special meal, or would you rather stay in and—?'

'Are you ready, babe?' Zach interrupted from the doorway slightly behind her, his deep voice slightly muffled. She turned her head to discover that he'd donned his gleaming helmet in her absence so that his identity was completely obscured. It also served to make him look several inches taller and even more impressive. 'Here, grab this and let's go,' he said, holding out the helmet he'd brought for her before turning his attention to the goggling man still standing in the open doorway. 'Sorry, mate, but fat old guys just aren't her thing, you know? So, if you don't mind…?'

There was more than a suggestion of a swagger in his walk as he strode directly towards her former colleague and for the first time Amy found herself battling the urge to giggle.

Quickly pulling the helmet over her head to hide the fact, she grasped the edge of the door again and widened it in a silent invitation for the man to leave.

'I told you I already had plans,' she said firmly, when he looked as if he was going to try to argue, and with the two of them advancing on him like extras out of a science fiction film he finally gave up and stumbled hastily out of her flat.

'I could come back later,' he began, clearly unhappy with the way his plans were being thwarted, but Zach advanced on him, looming over him in an almost menacing way.

'You do that, mate,' he invited with obviously false friendliness. 'But make sure you leave it at least half a century before you do because she's just not interested. OK?'

Amy managed to stay silent as they left the house, glad

she'd decided that she only needed to take her keys with her when she just managed to fit them in her pocket. There was no need for conversation as Zach directed her to climb on the back of the bike, neither did she need directions to wrap her arms securely around him, revelling in the fact that it was happening at last.

It wasn't until the powerful engine had roared into life beneath them that she allowed herself to chuckle aloud at what had just happened in her little hallway.

'Babe!' she snorted softly, feeling a renewed surge of response to the unexpected endearment. Who would have thought…?

'Well?' said a voice in her ear, and she gave a little shriek of shock.

'Hang on…babe!' teased Zach, his voice coming from the speaker that was part of the helmet he'd given her, but sounding so intimately close that it felt as if he was whispering in her ear. How could she have forgotten that he'd told her about the bike's sophisticated intercom system?

His deliberate repetition of the endearment made her laugh aloud.

'Well, you can hardly blame me,' he grumbled as he steered the machine between the slalom of cars parked on either side of her road. 'I was looking out of your window while I was waiting for you and I saw your slimy visitor arrive in front of the house. He didn't know it, but I watched him spray breath freshener in his mouth and try to suck in his gut as he walked up the path to ring the bell.'

There was certainly no spare gut on Zach's body. She could feel the taut muscles of his abdomen even through the thickness of his leather jacket.

'I had a choice,' he continued with a slightly rough edge to his tone that had nothing to do with their smooth passage out of the town and into the dark roads leading into the surrounding countryside. 'I could either come out into the hallway—incognito—and whisk you away, or…'

'Or…?' she echoed, suddenly realising just how much she was enjoying herself. It wasn't just the fulfilment of a long-ago fantasy, neither was it the fact that she had her arms around this virile man. It wasn't even the sensation that she was flying through the star-bright night. No, for the first time she was actually enjoying just being with a man, with no expectations on either side and…

'Or I could strip off my clothes before I dragged you into the sitting room, so that he'd know once and for all that you weren't interested… You aren't, are you?' he tacked on, but she nearly missed the question, every hormone she'd ever possessed suddenly clamouring for attention at the very thought of Zach stripping off. There certainly wouldn't be much need for him to *drag* her anywhere, and if that didn't give the lie to her earlier 'no expectations' thoughts, then…

'Oh, Lord, did I put my foot in it?' he groaned, throttling back. 'Would you rather have gone out with him than—?'

'No way!' Amy exclaimed hastily. 'I would be utterly delighted if I never saw the man again. He's married, for heaven's sake, apart from being a loathsome toad—with apologies to all toads worldwide for the comparison.'

It was Zach's turn to laugh and she not only heard the husky sound filling her helmet and her head but felt it through her hands over his stomach and through his chest where she was plastered against his back. In fact, the only way she

could have experienced his laughter any more intimately was
if they'd been…

'So, what's the story?' he prompted as he set the bike in
motion again, and somehow the fact that she wasn't having
to face him made the telling just that much easier.

'Nothing earth-shattering. Just a slimy married man seeing
a widow as fair game for his lechery…after all, we must be
panting for it now that we're not getting it from our husbands.'
Not that she'd ever had any regular attention from Edward
when he'd been alive. His progression up the ladder of
success had been far more important once he'd taken care of
the minor chore of securing an acceptable mate to carry his
eventual heir.

'But he was one of your superiors, wasn't he?' Zach
demanded, clearly incensed. 'Didn't you report him for
sexual harassment?'

'I didn't want to put his wife through that. She has enough
problems being married to the man. Anyway,' she added
lightly, 'by the time he was ready to progress beyond heavy
hints, I'd already decided to hand in my resignation. I was
lucky enough to land a job here, on home turf.'

Zach was silent for so long that Amy was sure she must
have bored him with her pathetic tale. These days, a career-
woman was supposed to be able to take care of herself in the
workplace, without resorting to crying foul when her male
colleagues stepped out of line. In spite of the fact that there
were now legal rules to prevent harassment, a woman who
reported such things could always be left with a black mark
on her record as a trouble-maker.

Absorbed by her thoughts, it took several moments before
she realised that Zach was slowing the bike and signalling

a turn, the engine muted now to nothing more than a throaty purr.

'Where are we going?' she asked, not recognising anything of their surroundings in the near-darkness.

'You'll see in a minute. Hang on,' he warned, before he accelerated gently down a rough track that seemed to lead directly into an impenetrable wall of greenery.

Amy gave a squeak as he plunged straight into it, burying her face in his back to avoid having her face scratched by the whipping branches, completely forgetting that she was protected by the visor on her borrowed helmet.

'It's safe to look now,' Zach teased gently, as the bike came to a halt, his voice lilting with laughter in her ears.

She peered over his shoulder and gasped at the beauty of the moonlit scene in front of them.

'Where are we? I've never seen this place before,' she murmured wonderingly, as she took in the way the moonlight caught the ripples on the river almost at their feet. The opposite bank was barely visible but shelved just as steeply as the one on their side, both banks lined with such thick greenery that it almost formed a secret corridor on either side to enclose the water.

She took off her helmet and shook out her hair, only then realising just how quiet and isolated this place was with the engine silenced. It was so peaceful, with only the soft sibilance of the passing river and the soughing of the breeze through the encircling trees surrounding them. They could have been the last people left in the universe, so great did their isolation seem.

'This is somewhere that I used to come when I needed to think,' he said softly when he'd removed his own helmet, as if he, too, was averse to destroying the peaceful scene. 'It was somewhere that no one could find me.'

'I wish I'd known about it when I was at school,' Amy sighed, remembering with a clench of remembered tension the unrelenting pressure to do well that had permeated the very fabric of her house.

'*You* didn't need anything like this—a place to escape to,' he scoffed. 'You had the perfect life of a princess.'

Amy snorted softly. 'That's what it looked like from the outside, did it?' She smiled wryly. 'Well, I suppose there were certain similarities, if you mean having to put up with your every move being organised and supervised by someone else—all for my own good, of course.' And if her parents had their way, that's exactly what her life would become again, now that she'd moved so close to them.

'I used to envy you,' she continued softly, remembering the independent young man he'd been, even as a teenager. 'You could do what you wanted, when you wanted and you *still* got good enough grades to go to med school.'

'Only because I spent so many hours studying…a lot of it just here, in fact…and even then I wouldn't have made it without your help.'

'*My* help?' Amy was startled. 'What help? We never saw each other outside school hours.'

He shook his head. 'If you hadn't been my lab partner, I doubt I'd ever have got good enough grades. In fact, I'm certain of it, because my essay work was dreadful.'

'But…' Amy frowned. There was something wrong here. That wasn't how she remembered things. Their teachers had all complained that if he'd only spend less time gadding about on his motorbike and more time on his written work, he'd get better marks, but Zach was saying that he *had* put in the hours of effort, so...

'I don't understand. If you were studying...'

Her tortuous thoughts were interrupted by the sound of someone or something crashing through the undergrowth a little way away from them.

Amy jumped and whirled to face in that direction, but there was nothing to be seen. It was far too dark and, anyway, she didn't really know what she was looking for.

Her biggest disappointment was that her train of thought had been interrupted, probably by nothing more than an animal going about its nocturnal business. And just when she'd felt as if she was about to discover a hidden truth about the man who had never left her thoughts.

'So...' She turned back to face him, hoping they could re-capture the reminiscent mood between them, but suddenly there were several angry shouts, this time from the other side of them. There was some more crashing about, seemingly all around them now, followed by several sharp cracks and the sound of something heavy falling in the water.

The next thing Amy knew was that she was on the ground, shoved off her feet and almost squashed flat by the weight of Zach's body landing on top of her.

Even though the impact had driven all the breath from her lungs, she instinctively started to struggle, trying to roll him off, but when that proved impossible she was struck by a sudden fear that something terrible had happened to him.

In a blinding flash of revelation she realised that the sharp sounds she'd heard could have been the sound of shots and blind terror seized her in a paralysing grip.

Zach! Had he been shot? Was he *dead*?

'Zach!' she keened breathlessly, redoubling her frantic efforts to roll him off. If he'd been shot, the damage might not be fatal yet. There could be something she could do to save his life…if only she could move him far enough off her to examine his injuries…stem the bleeding…

'Shh! Stay still!' he hissed right beside her ear, clamping a hand over each of her wrists to stop her struggles. 'I don't know who they are, but we're caught between them and we could get killed if they see us moving.'

'What?' she squeaked in disbelief, her brain unable to cope with the sudden switch from fear for Zach's life to relief that he was all right. To contemplate the prospect that *both* of them were in danger was a step too far.

'Shh!' he breathed again when she would have demanded an explanation, then silenced her in the most efficient way possible.

His lips were softer than she'd imagined all those years ago…and warmer…and, oh, so potent as he slanted them over hers, taking possession as though this was something that they'd done every day for years, rather than being the first time ever.

'Amy…' She felt his ragged groan reverberate through her, his broad chest pressing her more slender frame into the solid earth as she reached blindly to capture his mouth again. She'd dreamed of this for so long, and just in case this was nothing more than another dream, she was going to make it last as long as she possibly…

'Hey! Over here!' came a shout from close by, and the world reappeared around them. 'I've found a ruddy great bike hidden away, and there's… Oof!'

The owner of the voice obviously wasn't looking where

he was going because, before Amy had a chance to surface from that mind-blowing kiss, he'd fallen over the two of them and landed heavily beside them.

She heard a sickening crack and was wincing even as the man bellowed with pain.

'Don't move!' Zach ordered quickly, his voice cutting sharply over the man's curses. 'You've broken something.'

'No kidding!' the man swore caustically. 'Whatever gave you that idea?' But by that time Zach had knelt at his side, reinforcing his order with a restraining hand on the man's chest.

It took Amy several seconds longer to get her head in working order and before she could join Zach, several other burly figures encircled them in the darkness.

'Who are you and what are you doing here?' demanded one, as another figure shone a bright torch into Amy's face.

Amy threw a hand up to protect her eyes in the vain hope that she would still be able to see enough to help Zach with their unexpected patient. She was shocked speechless when her questioner grabbed hold of her arm and wrenched it un-ceremoniously behind her back.

'I said, who are you?' His threatening tone ended in a yelp.

Amy hadn't seen Zach move, but in the blink of an eye he was on his feet and had a choke hold on her assailant.

'Remove it or lose it,' he said in a dangerously quiet voice, and Amy breathed a sigh of relief as her arm was in-stantly released.

'Hey! You can't do that!' exclaimed one of the others.

'I can if you want your mate taken care of,' Zach growled, his tone unlike anything Amy had ever heard from him before. 'He's injured and we're both doctors. Whoever you're after, it isn't us.'

As if to underline his staccato sentences, there was a sudden commotion among the trees a little further along the river bank, and almost without another word being spoken they all set off in pursuit.

A groan at their feet brought Amy's attention back to the immediate task.

'If you're doctors, I hope you've got some king-sized pain-killers with you,' the man muttered as he struggled to roll over.

'I haven't got anything that would touch the sort of pain you're in,' Zach admitted candidly, once more preventing him from sitting up. 'I heard something go, and your collar-bone's intact, so it's either your arm or your shoulder.'

'Hell!' the man groaned through gritted teeth. 'Couldn't you have given me some good news instead?'

'The good news will be that you didn't break your neck, falling like that,' Amy pointed out, trying to ignore the throbbing in her shoulder after her recent rough treatment.

'And we won't be sure of *that* until we've seen an X-ray, so just lie still until we can get a paramedic here to put you in a collar,' Zach added. He turned to Amy. 'Could you get my phone out of my pocket and give them a call?' He leant away from her to give her access and she suddenly realised that the phone wasn't in his jacket pocket.

'Which pocket?' she asked as she picked her way around the injured man, grateful for the light thrown across the clearing by the abandoned torch that helped her to avoid treading on him.

'Shirt,' he said, and she wasn't certain whether she was relieved or disappointed that she wasn't going to have to do the clichéd hunt in his trouser pocket.

Not that her hormones were reacting any more sensibly with the fact that she could feel the firm slab of his pectoral muscle through the thin cotton of his shirt, and as for the heat radiating from his body…

'You'd better speak to them,' she said, as she pressed the button to connect the call. 'You'll be able to describe how to get here.'

Even as Zach was reporting their need for an ambulance, there was another sudden volley of shots and a shriek of pain.

'You'd better make that *two* ambulances and send the police,' he amended dryly before he cut the connection, and Amy wondered how he could be so cool while she was rapidly turning into a quivering wreck.

'Doc! Hey, Doc!' a voice called urgently from further down the bank. 'We need one of you here. Now!'

Amy met Zach's eyes, midnight dark in the limited light, and suddenly realised that he was concerned about leaving her unprotected.

'Go! I'll keep my head down,' she promised. 'Shout if you need me.'

He muttered something under his breath and with one last glance at the man groaning softly beside them loped swiftly into the darkness.

'We're water bailiffs,' her patient announced suddenly, startling her out of her concern for Zach's safety. 'There's been salmon poaching on this river…'

'Salmon poaching?' Amy gave a slightly hysterical giggle at the unexpected explanation for what had happened to destroy the peace of this beautiful spot. 'That sounds like something that happened in the Middle Ages.'

He gave an answering bark of laughter that ended in a

wince of pain as he inadvertently moved his arm. 'The difference is that these days it's big business…worth many thousands a year… And when they over-fish at the wrong time of year, they can wipe out the fish stock in a river so it never recovers.'

'Amy! I need you!' Zach called.

'Be still, my beating heart!' she muttered wryly under her breath, wishing that the first time he said those words to her had been under vastly different circumstances, and her patient laughed again.

'Promise me you won't move,' she demanded fiercely, knowing that Zach wouldn't have asked her to abandon the man if the situation hadn't been dire. 'If you've broken your neck and compromise your spinal cord, you could be paralysed for life.'

'Since you put it like that, I'll be good,' he said seriously. 'Go and help my mates… And keep your head down,' he called after her, and terror returned in a rush to remove most of the starch from her knees, almost dropping her in her tracks.

There were gunmen somewhere in the darkness, she reminded herself as she bent double and made for Zach's voice. If they saw her moving along the river bank, they might think she was one of the bailiffs and…

'Where are you?' she called shakily into the darkness as she started round a slight bend in the river and there they were, several torches illuminating a scene of carnage.

'There's two of them,' Zach said tersely. 'One with a gunshot wound. Are you wearing a belt?'

Before he'd even finished asking the question, her hands were at her waist, the spurting blood from an arterial bleed in the injured man's thigh obscenely bright in the stark glare of the high-powered torches. In the absence of any other means of slowing the blood loss, a makeshift tourniquet would be essential.

'Has anyone got some cloth—a clean handkerchief or something—to put pressure on the wound?' she demanded, as she threaded the leather under the wounded thigh. 'And I'll need a stick of some kind to tighten the tourniquet.'

A white shirt was thrust hastily in her direction and it was the unique mixture of soap and male musk that told her it had come from Zach, but there wasn't even time to look up and drool over his naked torso. If this man wasn't to lose a critical amount of his blood volume, she would have to work fast.

It seemed to take an inordinate amount of time to fold the donated shirt into a thick pad and to tighten the belt to keep it in place over the wound, but eventually she twisted the ligature tight enough to stem the flood.

'Hold this for me,' she demanded of one of the uninjured men, and a hand appeared to do her bidding, leaving her free to check the victim's pulse.

'How is he?' Zach demanded distractedly, clearly still struggling with his own unexpected patient.

'Bleeding under control with the tourniquet,' she reported, grateful for the reprieve. 'Pulse faster than I'd like and thready. He'll need some IV fluids before I have to loosen off the tourniquet to maintain circulation to his lower leg. What have you got?'

'Chest,' he hissed succinctly between gritted teeth. 'He dived in the river to escape and impaled himself on something. There are broken ribs…he's bleeding like a stuck pig…and his breathing's… Hell! I'm losing him!'

In the far distance, Amy heard the familiar sound of sirens with a lift of her heart, but this man couldn't wait even that long for help.

'I can't find a pulse,' she reported urgently, her fingertips searching for the reassuring thump of the carotid in the man's neck. 'He's arrested!'

'Breathe for him,' Zach barked, and as if they'd worked together for years rather than days he began to perform chest compressions while Amy counted and delivered the interspersed breaths.

From that point on, nothing else mattered than that they maintain the rhythm if their patient was to stand any chance of recovery, but it was only that thought that kept them going when it seemed as if it took for ever for relief to arrive.

'Right, mate, I'll take over,' said a hearty voice, and a figure in the familiar green uniform positioned himself to take over the exhausting job of pumping the unresponsive chest. The reassuring smile he threw Amy turned into an expression of surprise. 'Hey, Doc! Don't you get enough of this at work? Do you have to come out looking for it?'

CHAPTER SIX

AMY saw Zach sink back onto his heels, his chest heaving and his face gleaming with sweat. She knew only too well how badly every muscle must be burning after such sustained exertion.

When she realised that he was too short of breath to begin to report what had been happening, she began, even as another ambulance man was taking her place at the patient's head.

'Hi, Wayne,' she said, silently stifling a groan, knowing that this story—and her presence with Zach in this isolated spot—would be all around the hospital within minutes of the ambulance returning to base. 'There's a penetrating wound to the chest and broken ribs that may have pierced the lung. He started having breathing difficulties then went into cardiac arrest. Oh, and the injuries happened in the river, so there's probably water contamination in his chest, too.'

'How long has he been down?' Harry demanded as he set up the portable defibrillator to take a reading of the heart activity.

'For ever!' growled Zach, his breathing almost under control again.

'Almost twenty minutes,' supplied one of the water bailiffs in the background. 'Doc here wouldn't let us take over for him.'

'Stop compressions. Let's see what we've got,' came the order, and Wayne lifted his hands away from the ominously still body.

The machine whined to show it was working but they could all see the complete absence of any sort of convertible heart trace on the oscilloscope. This was one heart that wouldn't be beating again.

'Sorry, Doc,' said Wayne, all joking put aside. 'What do you want us to do?'

'There's nothing else you *can* do,' he confirmed quietly, although Amy could tell that he felt the same sort of impotent rage that always gripped her when they lost a patient.

'He *died*?' demanded a new voice in incredulous tones, and they all turned to look up at the young constable who'd been sent across to join them. 'How did he…? Oh… He's…' His eyes widened when he took in the scene and Amy knew just how gory it would look to the uninitiated as he played his torch over the body on the ground. Then he was whirling away, his torch falling from his hand as he retched violently into the darkness.

Amy got to her feet and approached him.

'First time?' she asked softly, when he'd finished heaving.

'God, yes!' he groaned. 'I never thought…' He propped his hands on his knees and shook his head. 'There's just so much blood! I wasn't expecting that.'

'Don't beat yourself up about it. It gets most people like that the first time—even doctors and nurses.'

'So how do *you* cope with it?' He cautiously straightened, as though uncertain whether his stomach would behave.

'You mean, as a mere woman?' she teased, and drew a pale smile from him that told her that he was going to be all right.

'Also, there's the fact that she happens to be an A and E doctor and sees this sort of thing all the time,' Harry volunteered cheerfully, as he began to stow away their equipment with the efficiency of years of practice.

His partner, Wayne, joined in. 'When I was training, I found it helped if I concentrated on what I was doing for the patient, rather than what it all looked like. So, in your case, you would need to…what? Take note of the surroundings? Make a list of the people present?'

Amy left him giving his pep-talk to join Zach beside the second victim, who was now festooned with IV lines connected to replacement fluids. She was relieved to see that her makeshift tourniquet had been removed and replaced with a pressure bandage, so she could put a stop to the silent clock that had been counting inside her head, monitoring the length of time that the leg had been deprived of proper circulation.

'I'll probably see you back at the hospital,' Zach was saying to the injured bailiff, a consoling hand on the man's arm. 'I'll be following the ambulances in, in case they need any further details.'

'Thanks, Doc—*both* of you!' he called back, as his stretchered form was being hurried towards the strobing lights of the nearest ambulance, probably unaware just how precarious his health had been before those vital fluids had started running into his body.

They both turned towards their final patient and as they hurried round the bend in the riverbank towards the second pool of light, Amy was startled to feel Zach's hand take hold of her own.

For a moment she wondered if it was just because he was concerned that she might stumble in the darkness—a darkness seeming all the more intense in comparison to the painful brightness of the lights over the third victim. Then he tightened his fingers in a deliberate squeeze.

'Are you OK?' he asked softly.

'Well, you certainly know how to show a girl a good time.' Amy chuckled and threw him a teasing glance, hoping he couldn't feel the way her pulse had rocketed at the contact.

Their help wasn't needed to load the final patient into the ambulance as he'd already been strapped to a stretcher with his neck and back protected by a stiff white collar and a spinal board and his arm supported across his body.

'Enjoy the rest of your evening,' the injured man called as he disappeared inside the ambulance. His voice was muffled by the oxygen mask, but the glint in his eyes told Amy that he hadn't forgotten the fact that he'd tripped over the two of them. Even with a healthy dose of analgesia taking the edge off his senses, he was probably well able to regale the paramedic with the facts as he saw them.

'You do realise that this story is only going to grow with the telling,' she groaned when there were only the able-bodied bailiffs and several policemen left on the scene.

'My reputation can only benefit from being pumped up into hero status,' Zach quipped. 'And the fact that I was with you…' He waggled lascivious eyebrows at her before sobering with a heavy sigh. 'If only we'd been able to do something for the bloke with the chest wound…'

'I was thinking about that…' Amy closed her eyes for a second, visualising the horrific injury analytically. 'We couldn't have left him in the water or he would have drowned, so leaving the branch in position wasn't an option either, as it looked as if it was still attached to the tree. And, anyway, the penetration looked as if it was at an upward angle. Do you suppose that it might have nicked the aorta or even hit the heart itself?'

'You mean, the reason why we couldn't keep his heart going was because there just wasn't enough blood left in the system?' He gave a single nod. 'That's entirely possible—it would make perfect sense, in fact—but we won't know until the post-mortem's done. I just wish…'

'I know.' She put a consoling hand on his naked arm then had to remove it quickly before she completely lost the thread of the conversation. It had been bad enough keeping her eyes off that expanse of muscular chest while there had been lives depending on their skills. Now that the crisis was over, there was nothing to stop her looking her fill, except sheer will-power. 'You don't like losing a patient any more than I do, but we both know that it's statistically inevitable.'

'Statistics!' he growled in disgust. 'Sometimes it seems as though the whole of medicine has been reduced to statistics and balance sheets.' He went to drag his hand over his head and suddenly froze with a look of horror on his face.

'Zach, what's the matter?'

'Gloves,' he ground out, holding both blood-stained hands up with their broad palms facing towards her. 'Neither of us were wearing any, dammit!'

Amy gasped as she looked at her own, similarly coated fingers. 'It just didn't cross my mind,' she admitted, thinking back to her first frantic efforts to stem the blood flow from the bailiff's thigh.

'Well, we both need to go straight back to the hospital and

get some tests done,' Zach said grimly, as he strode rapidly towards the bike and shrugged his way back into his jacket. 'I hope someone knows whether we have to get a court order to draw blood from the deceased.'

Amy honestly couldn't remember. She must have been told about the legal procedures during lectures on medical ethics, but as the possibility hadn't come up in a practical situation…

She donned her borrowed helmet and swung her leg over the back of the bike to slide up close behind him, overwhelmingly aware that there was a very different atmosphere between them as they prepared for the return journey.

That didn't mean that she couldn't appreciate the feeling of having her arms wrapped around him, but this time all the teasing that went with the start of a male-female relationship was gone. It was a far more urgent tension that permeated every muscle and sinew.

'Hey! Look at you two!' exclaimed Louella, when Zach escorted Amy into A and E a short while later. 'Harry and Wayne said we wouldn't believe our eyes when we saw the biker chick going out with our Zach!'

'Harry and Wayne will be lucky if I let them live beyond midnight,' Zach muttered under his breath, as he led the way into the closest empty treatment room and stripped his ancient leather jacket off Amy, before dumping his own on the nearest chair.

'Lordy! Were you hurt, too?' Louella demanded, all teasing gone when she caught sight of their bloodied hands for the first time.

'Not so far,' Amy said, trying to reassure her concerned

friend even as she tried to ignore the grim possibilities sprouting up like poisonous weeds in her own mind.

'Unfortunately, we didn't have any gloves with us when we got caught up in that little lot, and we've got two different lots of blood all over us.'

'Well, the first thing you need to do is get yourselves cleaned up,' Louella decreed, switching instantly to organisation mode. 'And I don't just mean washing your hands. Have a good hot shower, at least, and when you get back, we'll do all the other things that need doing. I'll have it all set up and ready to go.'

'I'd like to check up on those two bailiffs,' Zach began, but Louella shook her head.

'No, you don't,' she said firmly. 'They're both in good hands. The bullet wound is already in Theatre and the broken bones are on their way up to Orthopaedics to wait for a space in Theatre…probably first thing tomorrow morning.'

'But don't we need to—?'

Louella grabbed both jackets and thrust them into Zach's arms. 'All you've got to do is take care of yourself…and your biker chick!' she added mischievously.

Feeling almost like a child told to take her bath before bedtime, Amy meekly set off out of the department, her feet automatically heading for the nearest showers while she shuddered at the thought that she and Zach were now a juicy item of gossip.

'Here,' Zach said several minutes later, and thrust a fresh set of scrubs in her hands. 'So you don't have to put your clothes on again until you've had a chance to wash them.'

She stared up at him, silently mourning their disastrous outing. And it had started off so well.

There were shadows in his eyes, too. 'I'm sorry, Amy,' he said grimly. 'The last thing I intended was putting you in danger.'

'But you couldn't have known…you couldn't *possibly* have known that we would get caught between gun-wielding poachers and water bailiffs!' she exclaimed.

'But if I hadn't asked you to help me take care of them, you wouldn't be covered in blood that could be contaminated with HIV, hepatitis…'

'And you think that I needed to wait for your invitation before I jumped in?' she scoffed. 'Get real, Zach! This is what I do for a living, and we *both* forgot about the gloves because we could see that they needed help straight away, not when the paramedics arrived with a spare packet of disposable gloves!'

She pushed past him, marching furiously towards the door to the showers.

'Amy…' The hand that caught hold of her elbow was gentle but inescapable as he drew her back. 'That wasn't what I meant.'

'So, explain it to me.' She pulled her arm out of his grasp and was annoyed with herself when she immediately missed his gentle warmth, belligerently planting a fist on either hip. 'What did you mean?'

For a moment he said nothing, the rhythmically bulging muscles in his jaw telling her that he was probably grinding his teeth. His soft-voiced reply was a testament to his control.

'I meant that you were out with me, and that meant your safety was *my* responsibility, and if you'd been shot or you've been infected by a life-threatening disease—'

'Then it's because *I* made a choice of my own free will,'

she interrupted firmly, even as a strange warmth spread through her at his words. It couldn't just be because he felt responsible for her as her superior in the department, could it? Surely, there was something more…more *personal* in his concern?

Or was that just wishful thinking?

She was certainly guilty of *that* with his naked chest only tantalising inches from her, but it wasn't just his body that attracted her. It was the whole man, and she was having difficulty dragging herself away, even though she knew she ought to be cleaning the blood off herself.

'You did well out there, Amy,' he said. 'Much better than I did with my first GSW.'

His praise was an unexpected bonus, even though she didn't think she'd done enough to earn it.

'It was the first time I'd been confronted by one,' she admitted. 'And for it to happen almost in front of us, with absolutely no equipment to hand…I have no idea how you coped when you had half a dozen to deal with at a time. I take my hat off to you.'

To her surprise, the glaring overhead lights picked up the swift wash of colour that darkened his face and she wondered at his reaction. Had there been so few people to lavish praise on him or was it *her* approval that mattered more?

'Well, Louella's going to be waiting for us, so go and have your shower,' he said, but still lingered as though every bit as loath to end their time together as she was. When he added, almost as an afterthought, 'Do you want to go for a coffee afterwards?' she leapt at the suggestion.

'Cafeteria coffee while we wait to find out how the bailiffs have got on?' she teased, then decided to take a chance with a little honesty. 'If it's in your company, and is accompanied by ordinary everyday conversation, I accept.'

The surprise on his face almost had her wishing the words unsaid, but she couldn't back down now, not if she was going to find out if a relationship between the two of them was possible after all this time.

'Amy, dear! Where have you been? Are you all right?' demanded her mother, when the phone rang almost as soon as she got inside her door.

The frantically flashing light on her answering-machine told her that this was probably one of several calls she'd made, and Amy stifled a groan when she realised just what the messages would be about. The hospital grapevine had obviously outdone itself.

'I've been at the hospital and I'm fine, Mother,' she said in her most soothing voice. It didn't work.

'What do you mean *you're fine*?' her mother demanded with an edge of hysteria in her voice. 'You've been shot at! You could have been—'

'*No*, Mother,' Amy interrupted sharply. She really didn't want to have to deal with this now, but there was no option. 'I was *not* shot at. I just happened to be nearby when there were shots fired, but I was never in any danger.' Not with Zach spreadeagled on top of her to protect her...

'I would never have forgiven that man if anything ever happened to you,' her mother bulldozed on. 'And what on earth you were doing with him in the first place is beyond me. It was bad enough when you disappeared at that charity thing, but to spend any more time with him is just—'

'Mother, I work with Zach. All day. Side by side,' she

said, deliberately stretching the point. 'And we get on as well now as we did when we were at school together.'

'Well, that's as maybe, but I still don't understand why you'd want to see any more of him than that. And as for getting on that great dirty smelly motorbike of his—'

'Mother,' Amy interrupted again, her patience rapidly unravelling. 'You've spent months telling me I need a life outside my work and dragging me out to innumerable boring social functions. And just because you want grandchildren, you've wasted my precious free time while I'm bored rigid by yet *another* man with a calculator for a brain.'

'But, Amy—'

On the other end of the line it was her mother's turn to try to interrupt, but it was Amy's turn to be the bulldozer.

'Well, I don't know what lurid stories you've heard, but this evening I went out with a man…*willingly*…because I enjoy his company. Now, whether he'll ever be a candidate to sire all those grandchildren you want, I don't know yet…' just the thought of Zach siring her children was enough to turn her knees to porridge '…but it's really none of your business.

'Anyway,' she continued, metaphorically burning her bridges, 'you can't have it both ways. Either you want me to remain faithful to Edward for ever, or you want me to choose someone I can fall in love with and make a family.'

There was a strangely ominous silence from the other end of the line and a shiver ran up Amy's spine when she realised that her mother must have relinquished the phone and that she had just aimed her final salvo at her father.

'Young lady, that is no way to talk to your mother!' he roared, forcing her to pull the receiver sharply away from her ear for the sake of her eardrum.

For just a moment she almost reverted to the automatic submission that had been ingrained in her from childhood, but then a spark of pride had her firing back.

'Well, I'm sorry if you think I'm being discourteous, Father, but sometimes the two of you seem to forget that I'm a fully qualified doctor in my thirties, not a schoolgirl any more. I don't need the two of you watching my every move and I *certainly* don't need you organising my social life.'

'Well, you might be in your thirties, young lady,' he snapped belligerently, clearly incensed that she'd had the temerity to answer back, 'but you still haven't got any more sense than when you were in your teens if you've let yourself get tangled up with that Bowman character again.'

It was almost like entering some sort of science-fiction time warp, with her father laying down the law exactly as he had when she'd been a little girl.

Almost.

Except this time there was something inside her that told her it was finally time for her to follow her deepest instincts, even though they went completely against what her parents wanted.

'*That Bowman character*, as you call him, is actually a highly qualified accident and emergency specialist,' she said quietly, silently squashing the thought that she would have been equally well qualified if her career hadn't taken second place to Edward's. She had absolutely no idea whether there would ever be anything more than friendship between herself and Zach but...'He's someone with whom I have a lot in common and I enjoy his company—'

'Rubbish!' her father exploded furiously. 'You have absolutely *nothing* in common with that lout. And, furthermore, I have serious doubts that he—'

Amy reached the end of her tether and, for the first time in her life, quietly put the phone down on her father.

For a moment she contemplated leaving it off the hook so that he couldn't phone back, but her sense of responsibility wouldn't let her do it. If she were needed in A and E for a major incident, it was important that the hospital should be able to contact her, even though she wasn't officially on call.

'But I can turn on the answering-machine so I can screen my calls,' she muttered, suiting her actions to her decision just in time before the phone began to ring again.

Braced to hear her father's voice, she was certain her heart turned a complete somersault when it was Zach's deeper, sexier voice that filled the room.

'Uh, hi, Amy,' he said diffidently and a smile tugged at the corners of her mouth with the realisation that, at that moment, he didn't sound so different to the teenager she'd lost her heart to all those years ago. 'I just wanted to…to check that you're all right and—'

'You sound as if you hate talking to these things as much as I do,' she said, her breathless voice nothing to do with the fact that she'd had to walk all of three paces to reach the phone.

'Amy! You're there! When I heard the machine I wondered if you'd decided to go out.'

She could hear the smile wrapping around his words and felt an answering one stretching almost from ear to ear.

'No, I was using it to screen my calls.'

'You're having problems?' Now she could hear that the smile had dimmed, his tone full of concern. 'You're not being bothered by a stalker or something? Is it that slimy toad?'

'Nothing like that,' she reassured him quickly. 'Just

avoiding speaking to my father. The hospital grapevine's been at work and he's somehow got the idea that I got caught up in the middle of gang warfare.'

'I'm sorry. That's my fault,' he said. 'I shouldn't have—'

'Not that again! How on earth is it *your* fault?' she demanded crossly. 'Did you know the water bailiffs were going to be there? Did you know the poachers were going to be armed? For heaven's sake, it's bad enough having my father sounding off without you wearing a hair shirt!'

He was silent for so long that she began to wonder if he'd put the phone down on her, then she heard a husky chuckle from the other end.

'That told me!' he exclaimed. 'And all I really phoned about was to say…well, I enjoyed tonight.'

'In spite of the drama?' she managed, even though his admission made her feel as if she was floating.

'And in spite of the dreadful coffee,' he agreed with a chuckle. 'And I just wanted to ask if you were all right about everything…? I mean…'

'About what?' she prompted when he paused, wondering if he felt as uncertain about where all this was going as she was. 'The fact that our peaceful evening was ruined, that our bike ride was cut short or that I'm aching from head to foot— and no, you aren't allowed to take the blame for *any* of the above.'

'Well, if I'm not allowed to take the blame, how about if I take responsibility for trying to get it right next time?' he asked and her heart flipped into a double somersault.

'Next time?'

'I'm a man who likes to keep his promises, and I don't think that short jaunt counts as the bike ride we agreed on,' he announced. 'So, when are we both free again for an evening?'

Amy didn't know. She couldn't remember what her duties were, couldn't think much beyond the fact that the two of them were going out on his bike again and that she didn't want to wait any longer than absolutely necessary before they could spend some time together…alone.

'Unless you'd rather not?' he added, and she realised that he'd taken her silence for lack of interest.

'You can't get out of it that easily,' she teased, even as the more rational side of her brain was telling her that it would be more sensible not to put herself in danger again. 'If I'm going to be stuck with the nickname "Biker Chick" then I'm darned well going to earn it. Some parts of the evening were definitely worth repeating.' Even if every second of being plastered around his gorgeous body was a fight to control my hormones, she finished silently.

Such close proximity was going to test her powers of control to the limit, but she was determined to enjoy every minute.

CHAPTER SEVEN

WHEN a whole week went by without a single one of their shifts coinciding, paranoia began to creep in.

It didn't seem to matter how sternly she told herself that she was imagining it, all Amy knew was that she'd barely set eyes on Zach since their disastrous trip to the river.

They'd caught each other's eye several times at handover and she'd been almost certain that there was something more...something *special* in his expression since they'd worked together against the odds the other night.

Had she been seeing what she'd *wanted* to see?

Had he thought better of any involvement with her, no matter how platonic? Was he deliberately avoiding her? Or had her father somehow stuck his oar in?

'See? Paranoia,' she whispered to herself, knowing that there was no way that her father could have any say in the drafting of staff rosters, even if he became the chairman of the hospital board of governors.

Not that he wouldn't have liked to have that power, she admitted with a wince, remembering the last ear-blistering message he'd left on her machine.

Her mother had tried to pour oil on troubled waters by

inviting her for a meal one evening and Amy's feeling of guilt had almost made her give in until she'd remembered the latest in the line of chinless wonders she'd been slated to meet at the fundraiser. She had better things to do with her time.

'Like fight my way through traffic to get to the hospital on time,' she grumbled, as the lights turned against her yet again. It had been like this ever since she'd turned out of her own quiet cul-de-sac. She glared at the enormous supermarket lorry at the head of the queue. She'd been stuck in the queue of traffic behind it as it tried to manoeuvre its way along a street that had never been intended for anything so huge, and now it was completely blocking the junction ahead in all four directions.

She shared a commiserating smile with the young woman on the pavement beside her, three young children aged from about four to seven gathered around her as she waited for a safe moment to cross the road with them.

'Things that big ought to be banned from town centres,' Amy fumed as she put her car into reverse and took her turn to move back to give the lorry room to come back out of the intersection.

She set her brake and pressed the speed dial on her mobile to connect her to the phone in A and E, needing to warn them that she was definitely going to be late this morning. And she'd been looking forward to it, knowing that Zach was actually rostered for the same shift.

She was drumming her fingers on the steering-wheel while she waited for someone in the department to pick up the phone when she saw the driver immediately in front of her impatiently slam his vehicle into reverse and power his bulky four-by-four back towards her without even glancing over his shoulder.

Out of the corner of her eye she saw movement and with

a sudden sick feeling just knew that it was one of those little children.

Time seemed to stand still for several horrifying seconds but there still wasn't enough of it for her to slam a warning hand on her horn as the child darted off the pavement.

'No! Stop!' Her scream blended with the young woman's as her son froze in the middle of the road just seconds before the powerful vehicle slammed into him.

Amy was out of her car and running, the door left wide open as she sprinted towards the shiny vehicle that was still reversing, apparently oblivious to what had happened.

'Stop!' she shrieked again, slamming the side of her fist repeatedly into the vehicle's side panel as she dropped to her knees, dreading what she would see when she looked underneath the chassis.

'What the *hell* do you think you're doing? This is a new car!' snarled the owner, the door he flung open only just missing Amy's head in his fury.

'And that was a *child* you just ran over with it,' she shrieked back, barely sparing him a look, her eyes already focused on the ominously still figure crumpled on the unforgiving road.

One glance had been enough to tell her that even if he wasn't unconscious—or dead—he wasn't going to be moving any time soon.

'A and E staffroom,' said a voice in her ear, and she suddenly realised that someone had answered the *phone* call she'd placed before all this had happened.

'Amy Willmott here,' she said sharply. 'I'm involved at an accident. I'll be late.' She rang off and immediately dialled for the emergency services.

'Emergency. Which service do you require?' The female

voice sounded eerily similar to the one that had just answered in A and E.

'Police and ambulance,' she said crisply. 'A child's been run over by a four-by-four at the crossroads by the Royal George Hotel. The traffic's jammed by a supermarket lorry so tell them to come round from the by-pass end of the Shalford Road. I'm a doctor. I'll do what I can till they get here.'

Even as she'd been speaking she'd been edging forward on her knees, reaching under the vehicle to try to find a pulse, but her arm wasn't long enough. Having said all she needed to, she rang off and immediately lay flat in the road, barely sparing a grimace for her torn tights and ruined clothing in her efforts to determine the child's injuries.

There! A pulse!

'He's still alive, so far,' she muttered, and a keening cry of relief from somewhere behind her told her that the child's mother must be close enough to hear what she was saying. She would have to be more careful to keep her thoughts to herself, especially as she noted the growing pool of blood spreading underneath the lad's head and the trickle of fluid that had appeared in his ear.

His breathing was shallower than she would have liked, but he was still breathing unaided. Now, if only the light were better, she'd be able to check his eyes to see if they were equally reactive.

A quick inspection all around the area told her that the vehicle above her was high enough off the road that none of it was touching the child. In fact, as far as she could see, there was no reason why it couldn't be moved so that she could make a proper assessment of the youngster's condition.

She slid out again, the rough surface of the road snagging on her skirt again and dragging it halfway up her thighs before she could regain her knees and rectify the situation.

'You!' she snapped at the offending driver. 'Get in your car and drive it straight forward—slowly and carefully this time,' she added pointedly.

'But…' He blinked at the order, dithering over whether to do as she said and clearly shocked by what had happened.

'You're not supposed to move it till the police get here,' announced a bystander officiously, further confusing him.

'The vehicle isn't touching the boy, but there isn't enough room underneath it for me to be able to help him,' Amy said sharply. A sudden thought flashed through her mind and she delved in her pocket for her phone, glad that she'd taken the time to familiarise herself with its various functions when she was swiftly able to set it up to take several photos and a brief video clip of the situation.

'There, I've got a photographic record for the police, so you can move it—*now*,' she prompted urgently, only too aware that she still didn't know the full extent of the child's injuries. Impatience at his lack of instant action had her adding, '*I'll* move it, if you aren't capable.'

His male pride visibly dented, the man meekly climbed in and drew the car forward as far as he could go.

Amy didn't even bother waiting for him to switch off the engine before she was on her knees again.

'Oh, my God! Davey,' wailed his mother, clearly torn between her need to comfort her injured son and hang onto her terrified daughters.

As if in answer to the sound of his mother's voice, the child whimpered.

Amy felt a surge of delight at his response, but when he started to struggle, the vision of unstable neck injuries and the possibility of paraplegia had her reaching rapidly for him.

'Stay still, Davey. There's a good boy,' she urged soothingly, with one hand on his chest and the other on his forehead. 'You've had a bit of a bump and I just want to have a look at it. Don't move your head. Do you understand?'

There was only an unintelligible whimper when she framed his little face between her palms to stabilise his head and neck, but he wasn't struggling any more.

'I need some help here,' she announced, quickly realising that she couldn't hold him still and check him over at the same time. 'Has anyone had any first-aid training?' she demanded of the rapidly growing circle of bystanders.

'I have,' volunteered an outlandishly dressed teenager with an alarming number of facial piercings and purple-streaked porcupine hair. 'I did it at work, in case there were any accidents.'

'Good,' Amy said with a swift smile. 'What's your name?'

'Dee…well, it's really Deirdre, after my aunt.' She pulled a face that told Amy exactly what she thought of her given name. 'What do you want me to do?'

'Can you put your hands exactly where mine are, Dee?' Amy said, the quiet self-assurance in the young woman's eyes giving her confidence in the youngster's abilities completely at odds with her first impression.

'To stop him moving his head, in case he's injured his spine,' she said with a nod of agreement as she calmly curved frosted-blue-tipped fingers around the smooth childish cheeks.

'Exactly.' Amy breathed a sigh of relief that for all her

youth the girl was apparently unflappable. 'I'll have to do as many checks as I can without moving him. It looks as if it might be a while before an ambulance can get here.'

Even as she was speaking she was raising first one eyelid and then the other, noting with a sinking dread that the response of one was considerably more sluggish than the other. Was it evidence of bleeding inside the skull? If so, there was nothing she could do about it in the middle of the street. All she could do was catalogue her findings in her head so that it would save time when she handed the boy's care over to the paramedic when the ambulance finally arrived.

Amazingly, seven-year-old Davey didn't appear to have any obvious broken bones. In fact, he didn't seem to have *any* overt injuries apart from the obvious one to his scalp. But there was still that worrying trace of fluid from his ear that could signal catastrophic injuries within the brain.

Her mobile phone suddenly vibrated in her pocket and for just a moment she contemplated ignoring it.

'Yes?' It had better be something important or whoever had rung was going to find the call cut off without an explanation. At least it was hands-free.

'It's Ambulance Dispatch, here, Doctor,' said an efficient voice on the other end. 'They should be with you in about four minutes, now that they've got the police escorting them.'

Almost as he spoke, someone from the crowd called out, 'I can hear sirens! They're coming!'

Amy tilted her head to gauge the direction, pleased to hear that someone had passed on her advice about the best route to reach the scene. Now their biggest obstruction would be the crowd of people in her immediate vicinity.

'Can you all clear the way?' she called, raising her voice

so that it would carry over the concerned hubbub. 'Pedestrians, get back on the pavement and, drivers, back in your cars and move them as far over to the edge of the road as you can go. The emergency services will be here in three minutes and they need to come as close as possible.'

'Your car will need moving, too,' pointed out a young male voice behind her, and Amy looked up into the face from a mother's nightmares. 'I could do it for you, if you like.'

'That's Jonno, my boyfriend,' said the young first-aider, still calmly holding Davey's head. 'It's all right. He's passed his test and got a clean licence.'

'I've got a bike licence, too,' he added cockily, and Amy had to smother a smile when she realised that, apart from his shaven head and the piercings that matched Dee's, there was something about his attitude that reminded her of Zach, fifteen years ago.

'The keys are in the ignition,' she told him, silently sending up a prayer that her insurance company wouldn't have cause to slap her wrists for her nonchalance with the property they were covering. 'It's an automatic with power steering so it's a doddle to drive, but it's the three-litre version so go easy on the accelerator.' It hadn't been Edward's choice as a suitable car for the wife of an up-and-coming consultant—far too racy and powerful—but she'd loved it as soon as she'd seen its lipstick-red paintwork.

'No sweat!' He threw her a cheeky grin and strode eagerly to the open door.

It was time to check Davey's vital signs again and she was relieved to find that there had been no worsening of either his breathing or his pulse. Hopefully, that ruled out the possibility that there was any major blood loss from any internal injuries, but until he could be transported to the hospital she had no way of confirming whether the car had broken his ribs, leaving him in danger of a punctured lung or lacerated spleen or liver.

Out of the corner of her eye she saw young Jonno tentatively start to manoeuvre her car, but within moments he was driving it with almost the same confidence as she did, tucking it neatly into the tightest of spaces at the edge of the road to leave a clear path for the ambulance.

'I should have known I'd find you in the middle of things,' said a husky voice behind her, and Amy's heart thumped several extra beats when she looked all the way up his lean leather-clad body into Zach's dark eyes.

'Always there when I'm needed,' she joked with a slightly shaky smile, shocked to realise just how much she'd been longing to see him when her hands began to tremble with the need to be held in his comforting warmth. Treating patients in a fully equipped and staffed A and E was very different to coping alone in the middle of the road. She and Zach had made a good partnership that night by the river, but until his arrival here she'd been feeling very alone, with the sole responsibility for Davey's life.

'Anything I can do to help?' He bent down beside her and she was enveloped by the unique mixture of soap, leather and man that was uniquely Zach's.

'Ah, no.' She had to swallow before her voice worked properly. This was definitely not the time to lose concentration, especially if it was nothing more important than her over-active hormones causing her distraction. 'I don't think there's anything more we can do until the ambulance arrives.'

Even as she spoke, she caught her first glimpse of the

flashing emergency lights reflecting off the shop windows as they came into view round the corner, and within seconds they were pulling up just feet away from Davey's head.

'It's all right, Davey,' Dee said clearly, when her little patient grew visibly agitated. 'I've got you safe. That's just an ambulance siren. It's nothing to worry about.'

Amy was impressed that the youngster had realised how important it was to speak such comforting words to a frightened victim.

'You two are making a habit of this,' said Harry's familiar gruff voice as the paramedic dumped his bag of tricks beside him on the road and squatted at her side. 'What have you got for us this time?'

'Seven-year-old versus four-by-four,' Amy said succinctly, even as he took the appropriately sized cervical collar out of his bag and prepared to fit it to the child's neck, Zach positioning himself to assist. 'His pulse is sluggish, breathing is spontaneous and more or less regular but rather shallow. He's bleeding from a scalp laceration at the back of his head, but without gloves I didn't want to do any probing to feel for skull fractures.'

The blood of two patients on her unprotected hands had been enough to worry about for one week. She and Zach had both been relieved to be told that neither patient had carried any serious infections, but there was no guarantee that she would be as lucky a third time.

'There is a slight imbalance in the pupil sizes and response times and there's an apparent leak of CSF from his right ear. No other apparent injuries.'

'Did anyone see the accident? Do we know how it happened?' Harry prompted, clearly intent on gleaning as much information at the scene as possible.

'I saw it. It happened right in front of me,' Amy said grimly. 'The traffic was having to reverse to get out of the way of that delivery lorry.' She gestured over her shoulder towards the vehicle now totally stranded across the junction, unable to move in any direction. 'The car in front of me reversed without checking to see if the road was clear behind him and ploughed straight into Davey as he tried to cross the road.'

'Where was he hit? How did he fall?' Zach prompted, knowing as well as she did that different points of impact could result in widely different injury patterns.

Amy closed her eyes for a second to visualise those important seconds. 'He'd run into the road and must have realised at the last moment that the car was coming back at him because he was facing the vehicle almost straight on when it hit him. He fell straight back, striking the road with the back of his head while the wheels passed him by on both sides.'

'At least it was a blessing that none of the wheels caught any of his limbs,' Harry said darkly. 'Those things are so big and heavy that the level of damage they do usually means amputation.'

Between them, Davey was soon strapped safely to a backboard and on his way into the ambulance ready for his mother to join him for a swift journey to hospital.

With a sudden attack of guilt, Amy realised that she'd almost completely ignored Davey's mother, both while she'd been monitoring the child and then when she'd been handing over to the paramedic. She turned to look for her, wondering how on earth she'd been coping with the situation with two small girls clinging to her.

She needn't have worried. Jonno was sitting on the edge

of the kerb with one little girl on each knee, the older one examining the chunky silver anchor dangling from his ear and the younger one grinning in delight as she tentatively ran delicate fingertips over the emerging bristles on his shaven head. Davey's mother was sitting beside him, wrapped in his voluminous jacket, while the tears streamed down her face, her eyes never leaving her little son.

'Thank you,' Amy said as soon as she reached Jonno, the words heartfelt.

'No. Thank *you*,' he countered with a self-deprecating shrug as he gently stood each little girl on her own feet and rose to his. 'It would have been years before I got a chance to drive one of those if you hadn't trusted me.' He handed her the keys then turned to help Davey's mother to her feet.

'Whoops!' said Zach, arriving just in time to catch her when she wobbled precariously on shaky legs. 'The paramedic wants to know if you're coming in the ambulance with Davey.'

'Can I?' she implored, gazing up at Zach with eyes drowning in fear. 'And the girls?'

'And the girls.' He released her to stoop down and scoop one up in each arm. 'They'll be off as soon as they've got you all safely inside.'

The meaningful nod of his head and his decisive strides told Amy that they needed to get moving as soon as possible and her heart sank. Was Davey's condition deteriorating? Had she missed something important? Something life-threatening?

It was Jonno who escorted the shaky woman to the vehicle, only accepting his jacket back when Harry produced a blanket to replace it. Then, with the lights flashing silently this time, the driver made short work of turning the vehicle in spite of the restricted space, and they were away.

The siren came on again just before they turned the corner and disappeared out of sight, and Amy could only imagine what was going on inside.

'Will he be all right?' Dee asked quietly, then shook her head and answered for herself. 'Stupid question. How could anyone know until they'd done X-rays and stuff? But…how long will it be before you'd know?'

'Not until the results of all the tests are through, and sometimes not even then,' Zach said matter-of-factly. 'Sometimes in A and E we just have to clean a patient up and they're virtually ready to go home, and sometimes they can be weeks in Intensive Care, making no progress at all before they start to improve. Others aren't so lucky.'

'So, if I rang the hospital, could I find out how he's doing?' she asked, directing this question at Amy.

She shook her head. 'The hospital wouldn't give out that sort of information to someone who isn't even family, but… Look, give me your phone number and I'll see what I can do.'

'Thanks. Thank you very much.' Amy noticed that her smile was a little shaky now that the immediate drama was over, a common reaction in the aftermath of a sudden surge of adrenaline.

'You did very well, Dee,' she said, putting a consoling hand on the young girl's arm, the tremors more obvious under her clothing. 'If you ever consider a change of career, I think you ought to consider medicine. You kept your head beautifully.'

'And wasn't Jonno brilliant with the little kids?' Dee exclaimed, and Amy had to hide a smile when the young man's resulting blush travelled right up over his shaven head.

'I didn't really do anything,' he said with a shrug, as he donned his over-sized jacket again. 'I was only distracting them so they weren't looking at their brother lying there.'

'And you took care of their mother,' Zach added quietly, holding out his hand towards the younger man. 'You did well. You've got good instincts about caring for people.'

Jonno tentatively shook his hand as though it was something he didn't do very often, and mumbled something unintelligible as his blush intensified.

'Excuse me. I'm PC Frostic. Which one of you is the doctor?' interrupted a voice, and they all turned to face a young uniformed policewoman.

'Two of us are,' Zach volunteered helpfully. 'I'm Dr Bowman and this is Dr Willmott.'

'Well, which one of you was it who rang the incident in? If you were a witness, we're going to need a statement.'

'Will it take long? Only I was due at work…' Amy glanced down at her watch and gasped. 'I was due to start my shift over half an hour ago in A and E.' She glanced around her at the chaos that still surrounded them. 'How long is it going to be before this lot is sorted out?'

'Are you both due on duty?'

'Yes, and the department's short-staffed at the moment,' Zach said. 'We really don't have time to—'

'Just a minute, Doctor,' she said, raising her index finger, and turned away to speak into the neat gadget that had recently replaced the old bulky walkie-talkies. Less than a minute later she turned back. 'I've just cleared it with the DCI. We can do your interview later, so you're free to get to work…if you can get out of this tangle.'

'Mine's the red one over there,' Amy said with a grimace,

when she saw the way it had become completely hemmed in. It would be ages before she could get away.

'Mine's the Honda Fireflash abandoned halfway down the road. I could give you a lift, Amy,' Zach offered.

'But my car…'

'Is the car locked, Doctor?' the young policewoman interrupted. 'If you'd trust me with the keys, I could make certain it was delivered to the hospital for you.'

As Amy handed over her keys again, she couldn't help noticing that there was the same avid expression on the officer's face that there'd been on Jonno's at the prospect of driving her car.

'You could always give me the keys back when you come to do the interview,' she suggested with a conspiratorial grin.

'I could do,' PC Frostic agreed eagerly, returning the grin whole-heartedly as she tucked the keys in her pocket. 'I'll see you later, then, Dr Willmott.'

'Now, where's this…what did you call it?' she asked Zach as they set off through the tangle of cars and official vehicles.

'Honda Fireflash. This is it,' he supplied, as he stopped beside the sleek mixture of bright polished chrome and immaculate paintwork that almost exactly matched the scarlet of her car in daylight.

'It's your motorbike,' she said stupidly, only now realising the significance of his leather clothing. Then she looked down at the remains of the neat suit she'd donned that morning. It was dirty and ruined beyond repair but, more importantly, it had a slim straight skirt that made it totally inappropriate for riding a motorbike. 'I can't get on that thing!'

'You did before,' he pointed out blandly, as he retrieved two helmets from the panniers then rocked the bike off its stand and prepared to throw his leg over it, but he couldn't hide the wicked gleam in his eyes.

'You know very well that I was wearing trousers the last time!' she exclaimed, unwillingly cradling 'her' helmet. 'I'd have to…' She clamped her lips shut, but he finished the thought for her.

'You'd have to pull your skirt right up to your…hips?' he suggested, wickedly changing the word they both knew he was thinking. 'Well, if you sit really close to me, no one will be able to see anything untoward. And, anyway, it's only for a couple of minutes until we get to the hospital. Then you could change into a scrub suit without anyone being any the wiser.'

It was logical. It was sensible. But the gleam in his eyes had grown brighter and she knew that he was every bit as aware as she was that until they arrived at the hospital she was going to be pressed against his back with little more than her underwear between them.

Not quite, she silently corrected herself as she surrendered to the unavoidable, awkwardly clambering into position behind him in a vain attempt at preserving her modesty, then giving in to the inevitable and sliding right forward so that she was plastered against his back. There was nothing between them but her underwear and the supple leather that, rather than being cold against her thighs, was warm from the heat of his body and fitted him like a second skin.

CHAPTER EIGHT

'NO ONE will be any the wiser? Ha!' Amy muttered, her cheeks burning for the umpteenth time that morning.

It would have been true if the department was as busy as usual, but with a major traffic hold-up blocking half the access routes into town, far fewer than the usual number of casualties had arrived for the Monday morning rush, so half the department had been standing idle when Zach had drawn up outside the main entrance.

The pleasure of wrapping her arms around him again and feeling the rush of air as the powerful engine sped them swiftly to their destination had almost made her forget that her legs must look completely naked with her skirt hiked almost to her waist.

The first wolf whistle had reminded her with a jolt, as had the impossibility of dismounting without revealing both the colour and the brevity of her underwear.

And Zach hadn't helped a bit.

Even with his visor down on his helmet she'd been able to see the searing glance that had taken in her unintentional revelation as he'd murmured, 'Have you got a thing for scarlet, then?' through the intercom. By the time she'd dragged her helmet off and marched into the building, her cheeks had matched them.

And, of course, the hospital grapevine had ensured that the tale had only grown with the telling. Just moments ago, she'd heard one of the paediatric consultants, visiting the department to take a look at a hypoglycaemic seven-year-old, asking Louella if it was true that one of the A and E staff had turned up that morning wearing nothing more than a bra and a G-string.

'If my parents hear *that*,' she groaned, and threw her coffee down the sink, unable to force any more of it into a stomach that was twisted into knots.

The phone beside her rang.

'A and E staffroom,' she said, her throat tight with tension, and as if her thoughts had conjured it up, she heard her mother's voice in her ear.

'Can I speak to Dr Willmott, please?' she demanded abruptly, the edge to her tone telling Amy that the story *had* travelled that far…but which version of it? Was it just the one that had her arriving late for her shift, the 'biker chick' on Zach's motorbike, or had things progressed beyond the G-string now?

Amy closed her eyes and drew in a steadying breath. She had no idea what she could say that would mollify her status-conscious parents. The only thing she did know was that she didn't want to speak to either of them while she was standing in the A and E staffroom where anyone could walk in at any time.

'I'm sorry, but she's with a patient,' she said in a patently false Scottish accent. 'Can I take a message?'

'No, you can't,' snapped her mother, and Amy was able

to judge how upset she was when she only just remembered her manners in time to say, 'Thank you for offering,' before she rang off.

'I'm a coward,' she said dismally, when she realised that she was now avoiding speaking to either of her parents.

Her father had stopped leaving messages, but her caller ID was telling her that he was still ringing her several times a day in the hope of catching her unawares. Her mother was resorting to more direct methods, if this latest call was a sample. How long would it be before she actually turned up in the department and demanded an account of Amy's shaming behaviour?

The door swished open and she forced herself to straighten up, determined that no one would see just how much all this was getting her down.

'There you are, Amy!' exclaimed one of the most junior nurses. 'Louella sent me to deliver this.'

This was a small padded envelope bearing the familiar logo of one of the major drug companies.

'Shame it isn't anything exciting,' the young woman commiserated as she turned to leave the room. 'It's probably nothing more than some free samples of their next wonder drug, to persuade you to prescribe it.'

Amy would probably have thought the same, if the drug companies were in the habit of targeting the lower orders in the department, and if she hadn't noticed that the packet had already been opened once, and the replacement label on the front hadn't been addressed to Dr ABC Willmott.

'Zach,' she breathed, fighting a smile even as she fought with the tape holding the flap secure, not completely certain whether she should be throwing the thing away unopened or opening it extra-carefully. Would it be something that would cheer her up or something that would depress her still further?

Gingerly, she peered inside and drew out a folded piece of paper.

'I'm sorry. I wouldn't have embarrassed you deliberately,' said the brief note in the unexpectedly flamboyant handwriting that had fascinated her from the first time she'd seen it. 'I hope the enclosed will help. Zach.'

She shook the small package to tip out the contents— something tightly folded and made of a slippery pink fabric that immediately began to unfold itself until it was draped in all its glory across her hand. It was a pair of the baggiest, ugliest 'old lady' knickers she'd seen in a long time, easily large enough to reach all the way from her waist to her knees.

'Harvest festivals.' She chortled as she held them up and laughed aloud at the memory of the first time she'd heard the term applied to this particular style of underwear—by Zach, of course. 'All is safely gathered in,' she quoted, her heart immeasurably lighter for the teasing gift.

Not that it had solved the problem with her parents, or would do anything to make the rampant gossip die down, but it had certainly put her in a better frame of mind.

'From now on, it'll all be like water off a duck's back,' she murmured bracingly, as she deposited Zach's gift in her locker and set off to do battle with the increasing numbers of people waiting for attention.

To her annoyance, she discovered that her determination was effective only as long as their colleagues would keep their minds on the job.

'Why didn't you tell me you were into bikes, Amy?' murmured the radiographer, while they were positioning a patient for the first of a series of X-rays after a spectacular fall off a ladder. 'I'd have gone out and bought one, specially.'

'Did you buy the underwear locally, or is it one of those specialist catalogues?' an avid staff nurse asked, her voice just a shade too loud for the question to be confidential. 'Do they do all those whips and chains and things, too?' she added into the sudden silence, and Amy had to bite her tongue, hoping that discretion *was* the better part of valour when she refused to be drawn into replying.

The situation wasn't helped by the fact that, whenever someone made such a comment, Zach was always in the vicinity and she only had to look at him to remember how it had felt to be pressed that close against him, every inch of her revelling in the lean muscular warmth wrapped in supple leather.

And when Louella joined in with an 'It's about time, girl!' and a lascivious wink, she didn't know where to look, especially when she saw the gleam of laughter in Zach's dark eyes.

'Don't let it get to you,' he murmured, under the cover of a volley of instructions as their next patient was handed over by the paramedics, who'd scooped him out of an excavation at a building site. 'Keep smiling mysteriously. It'll drive them all nuts.'

'If *I* don't go nuts first!' she muttered back, as she reached out for the phone, her instincts telling her that it would be a good idea to find out how long it would be before there was a theatre free.

'Here, will you check off the calculations for the dosages?' he said, holding out the clipboard.

'I was just going to phone up to Theatre to find out how soon we can send him up,' she explained.

'I'll do that,' he offered, taking the phone out of her hand, his eyes focused on the team's progress as they hooked the patient up to all their high-tech monitoring equipment.

Amy didn't think much of it at the time, but later, when she was sitting in front of a pile of paperwork, checking laboriously that the written records were clear and that they accurately documented exactly what had gone on according to her own notepad full of jottings, she realised that it was something that had happened several times recently.

Was it just a coincidence, or was it a crafty way for Zach to avoid doing his share of the paperwork?

She didn't honestly believe that the conscientious doctor she'd come to know over the last few weeks would really be shirking, but the thought niggled at her at intervals throughout the rest of her shift. It brought to mind the memory of their days as lab partners in school when he'd done almost exactly the same thing—he'd always been the one who'd performed the experiments they'd been set while she'd been the one who'd acted as scribe, taking down the results.

Not that she'd minded at the time. She'd been so delighted to be his lab partner that she'd have been quite happy to do *all* the work, as long as she'd been able to be with him.

Well, she might be rapidly falling head over heels in love with him all over again, but she wasn't that naïve teenager any more and she had more than enough paperwork of her own to do.

It was Zach's misfortune to walk in to the room while the thought was fresh in her mind.

'Coffee?' he offered breezily, his own hands remarkably free of any piles of files.

'Coffee and conversation,' she agreed, and there must have been something in her tone to put that suddenly wary expression on his face.

'Any particular topic?' he prompted, as he doctored the steaming brew just the way she liked it, with a hefty dash of milk and the tiniest bit of sugar.

'Paperwork,' she said pointedly, as she closed the manila cover of one file and moved it to the completed pile before opening the next. 'Have you got much to do, or does your clever ploy shift it all on to everyone else?'

The wary look was gone instantly, hidden behind the blank wall he'd worn every time one of their teachers had started berating him.

He carried the two mugs over and set one down in front of her, then paused infinitesimally before he sat himself down in the chair beside her. He was silent for several long seconds then sighed heavily, his shoulders hunched defensively, just as the younger Zach's had.

'I'm dyslexic,' he said quietly, and disbelief took her breath away, leaving her speechless. 'I do my share of paperwork, but I have to take my time over it without any interruptions to make sure I don't make any mistakes.'

'But...' She shook her head. 'You never said anything at school.'

'I didn't know when I was at school,' he said simply. 'The teachers labelled me as a trouble-maker and washed their hands of me, and I didn't know why things didn't make sense, so I didn't know how to ask for help.'

'But...you passed all your exams. You even got high enough grades to get into medical school...and all the way through.' She still couldn't take in the enormity of it. It was almost too fantastic to be true, but if so, it made so many of the pieces to the puzzle called Zach Bowman make sense.

'I passed my exams at school because you helped me,' he said simply.

'Me?' She was stunned. 'What did *I* do when I didn't even know you had a problem?'

'You were my lab partner for all the science subjects—the ones I needed the highest grades on to get my place at med school. It was because you were willing to be the scribe for all the lab work, giving me your neatly written account of all the experiments so that I could copy them out, that I was able to keep up. The rest of it was just endless hours of study, going over and over everything until I could make sense of it to put some sort of answers together for the final exams.'

'That's incredible,' she breathed, hardly able to comprehend the level of dedication it had taken for him to have done the same thing all the way through medical school. Her admiration for him was growing by leaps and bounds.

'My marks were never brilliant on the written exams, but once one of my tutors spotted several tell-tale mistakes in them she was able to get me sent for assessment and I was given a little extra time in the exam room. But I absolutely aced the vivas!' He chuckled. 'I had to study so hard for the written exams that there was no way they could trip me up in an oral one. That brought my marks up every time.'

'So you try to get someone else to do the writing for you—'

'Usually only in high-pressure situations when there isn't time for me to double-check myself,' he interjected quickly.

'And then you catch up with the rest of the paperwork when you *have* got time.' She shook her head. 'You're an amazing man, Zach Bowman. When I think of the number of people I've met who've used a diagnosis of dyslexia as an excuse for failure or for not even bothering to try…'

'The person who did my assessment in my first year at med school was a fellow sufferer who'd ended up with a PhD and specialised in treating learning difficulties. He told me that there's nothing wrong with my brain or my intelligence. It's just wired up to perform differently to other people, and once I worked out the best way to manage my idiosyncrasies there should be no stopping me.'

'I never dreamed…' She shook her head again, still unable to believe it. 'I knew just how bright you were, in spite of Mr Venning calling you thick and stupid. It just never would have occurred to me to think that you were dyslexic.'

'Some people still won't accept that there is such a condition, putting the problem down to bad teaching at a critical stage, or missing something important through illness, or moving from one school to another, or just a pseudo-scientific excuse for badly behaved children, but there are so many who don't fall into any of those categories and have a distinct set of anomalies, some correctable and some that you just have to develop coping strategies to stop them messing up your life.'

'Such as getting a colleague to check your written work, or getting them to do the writing when it needs to be done quickly,' Amy finished for him, the explanation so obvious now that she knew the situation. She gazed at him in awe, still hardly able to comprehend the level of dedication it had taken for him to achieve all that he had. A crazy sort of pride filled her heart to overflowing. She'd respected him before, but now her admiration knew no bounds.

'Are you going to say anything?' he asked, with a strangely tentative edge to the question.

'About what? To whom?' she countered with a shrug. 'You're a fully qualified doctor. What more does anyone need to know?' They certainly don't need to know that I've probably fallen even deeper in love with you, now that I know just what you're capable of, she added in the secrecy of her head, sorry that she hadn't attended the same medical school so that she could have made the mammoth task of so much study a little easier.

The envelope was just one of the handful Amy received at home each day, and she opened it quite cheerfully between mouthfuls of warm buttered toast topped with the bitter sweetness of Seville orange marmalade.

Her smile disappeared entirely when she read the contents, advising her to phone the above number for an appointment to have a second Pap smear done as the results of the first had been inconclusive.

'Inconclusive?' A black cloud of dread descended over her. This was definitely one of those times when a medical education *wasn't* the best thing. She knew only too well exactly what those careful words concealed—the fact that they'd seen some abnormal cells among those taken from her cervix, and needed another sample to determine whether she had cancer.

'Cancer!' she whispered through a throat grown tight with fear, instantly convinced that the cells had already progressed through the pre-cancerous stage to the full-blown disease.

Would it be in the early stages, where the growth could be

removed without leaving her unable to carry a child, or was it already too late for that, with a radical hysterectomy her only option if she was to live?

Her fearful mood wasn't improved when her first patient of the morning was a woman in her late thirties who had collapsed in the bathroom that morning and had been brought in by her husband—much against her wishes.

'We only got married a month ago,' Francis Paxman said, clearly beside himself with worry but trying to make light-hearted conversation. 'I've been trying to persuade her to make an honest man of me for nearly fifteen years, and as soon as we get back from our honeymoon, this happens.'

Jane Paxman looked positively grey as she lay back against the pillow and when she opened her eyes to meet Amy's, there was such a strange expression in them. She'd seen something like it before, in the eyes of a trapped animal who had lost all hope.

But that couldn't be true, surely? Not in someone who'd finally married the man she'd known for over fifteen years.

Anyway, even if the woman *was* regretting her decision, that shouldn't be enough to cause such a collapse. There was something more going on here.

'Mr Paxman, if you would wait outside for a few minutes…while we do a few tests,' she suggested, needing to ask a few questions that couldn't be asked while he was sitting there, clinging to his wife's hand. 'The nurse will show you to the relatives' room and get you something to drink.'

'A double brandy would go down well,' he joked, as he reluctantly released his hold. At the last moment he bent forward and pressed a swift kiss to his wife's cheek, his own growing red at the fact he'd done it in front of an audience.

'I love you, Janey,' he whispered, and hurried out of the room, redder than ever.

'Mrs Paxman,' Amy began, then paused to take his place in the seat beside her and took the slender bloodless hand between her own. 'Janey,' she began again gently. 'I get the feeling that you know exactly why you collapsed this morning. Are you going to tell me what's going on?'

For a long time there was no reply but then slow tears began to trickle from the corners of her eyes. Amy waited, somehow knowing that this time it was important to be patient even as she was supplying the paper hankies to the silent woman.

Finally, Jane drew in a shuddering breath and opened her eyes and that awful expression was clearer than ever.

'I'm dying,' she whispered.

Amy wished she had a coin for every time a patient had said that to her, but this time she believed it without question.

'What's wrong with you?' she asked, but with a deep shiver of dread she suddenly knew even before the deathly pale lips formed the word.

'Cancer.'

'Where, and when were you diagnosed?' She didn't bother with the usual hearty disclaimers, knowing they were worthless. This woman *knew* what was killing her.

'Ovarian. It had metastasised before I even went for tests. It had already spread so far that there was nothing they could do.'

'Not even chemo or…?'

Jane Paxman shook her head wearily. 'Nothing. They couldn't even tell me that the treatment would give me any extra time, so there wasn't any point in making a misery out of whatever time I had left.'

'And your husband doesn't know?'

'I couldn't tell him,' she breathed, her eyes screwed tight as she fought the tears. 'We've loved each other for ever and it was almost a joke between us that he kept proposing and I kept putting him off. Then…*this*…' A sob escaped her control and it took a minute or two for her to regain it.

'So the next time he asked, you accepted,' Amy guessed.

'On condition that the marriage took place as soon as it could be arranged. No months and months of planning. No big celebration. Just him and me and…and it was beautiful and he was so happy and…and…I just felt so *guilty* because I felt as if I was cheating him. He should have known what was happening *before* he was tied to me, but I was afraid that if I told him, he might not want…'

'But you know him too well for that,' Amy said with a flash of understanding. 'In your heart, you knew that he would marry you any way he could have you, and this was the only way you could see of making your wedding a happy occasion. A memory he could take out and cherish after you were gone.'

'But it's happening too *soon*,' she wailed weakly. 'I haven't had enough time to work out how I'm going to tell him, and I've got to do it *now*.'

'Do you want me to do it for you?' Amy offered, a glance at the various monitoring displays confirming that her patient was stable enough for her to leave her long enough to do that for her.

Jane took several moments to think about it and Amy could tell that the idea was tempting, but the determination in the way the woman pressed her lips together told her that the offer was going to be rejected.

'Thanks for the offer, but this is something *I* have to do,' she confirmed. 'If you could bring him back in?'

'He'll only start grilling me if I go to get him,' Amy pointed out as she reached for the phone.

'Louella, I'm in Resus Three with Mrs Paxman,' she said as soon as she recognised the Caribbean accent, the fact that her colleague had already arrived for duty telling her just how much time had elapsed. 'Fleur's with Mr Paxman in the relatives' room. Could you get her to bring him back in here?'

'You got a problem there, Amy, girl?' Louella asked softly, obviously picking up on something in Amy's voice.

'No problem,' Amy said equally softly.

'Tell me later. I'll send Mr Paxman in.'

By the time the worried man pushed his way through the doors, Amy had cleared the room of all the other personnel, sure that this conversation was going to be difficult enough for Jane without a cast of thousands listening in.

'Janey! Sweetheart, are you all right? Have they found out why you collapsed this morning?' The lump in Amy's throat grew as she turned away to give them some semblance of privacy, concentrating hard on tasks that she could usually complete without thinking about them. This man obviously loved his wife. He was going to be devastated when she told him how little time they had left together.

'*No!* Oh, Janey, no! It's not true. It *can't* be…'

Amy threw a quick glance over her shoulder to confirm that the monitor readings were still within normal bounds. Blood pressure was raised, as was pulse rate, but that was hardly a surprise with the stress Jane was under, even with her husband's arms wrapped right around her, cradling her as though she was the most precious porcelain figurine in the world. His shoulders were shuddering with the force of his sobs as she apologised over and over again.

With the force of an express train it suddenly hit Amy that *this* could be what *she* would be going through in just a few months' time, but in her case there would be no supportive husband mourning a life cut short. She had colleagues and friends aplenty but, apart from her parents, there would be no one to hold her close while she cried out her fears and regrets for all the things she would never achieve.

So why did Zach's image burst into her mind?

He wasn't her husband or her lover. In fact, in spite of the new relationship they had been forging since they'd started working together, he was little more than a friend, no matter what her dreams might imply.

'Excuse me?' Mr Paxman's voice broke into her thoughts and she wondered guiltily exactly how long she'd been gazing blankly at the wall. 'What happens now? Can I take Jane home?'

'Her oncologist has been paged and will be on his way down. He'll be able to tell you what's been going on to make Jane collapse this morning and discuss with you what that means as far as treatment goes.'

'I'm *not* going to be admitted,' Jane said as firmly as her weakened condition would allow, her voice choked by emotion. 'I want…we *both* want for me to stay at home as long as…' She couldn't finish the sentence, but Amy didn't need the words.

'If you've already discussed that with Mr Khalil, he'll have it in your notes. If not, it would probably be a good idea for the two of you to go up to the oncology ward—'

'But she doesn't want to be admitted,' her husband interrupted swiftly.

'And she won't be, unless it's absolutely necessary,' Amy promised. 'It's just that it'll be a bit quieter and more private than down here.' She risked a gentle joke. 'Don't worry, the bed shortage is still severe enough that they're unlikely to start forcing people to stay.'

They both smiled, but when the door was shouldered open by Mr Khalil, it was short-lived.

'Jane, how are you?' he asked, as he hurried across the room to her, taking one of her hands and pressing it between both of his. 'And this must be Francis.' He offered a hand to her husband, his large dark eyes full of sympathy. 'Jane has told me so much about you that I almost feel as if we've met before.'

He returned his gaze to his patient. 'You're not looking quite as radiant as I was expecting,' he teased her gently, then surprised Amy by adding, 'Has it been a rather…energetic month since the wedding?' with a waggle of his eyebrows and made both Francis and Jane chuckle, a wash of embarrassment lending a welcome touch of colour to Jane's pale cheeks.

The apparent suggestiveness of the oncologist's gesture had been so at odds with his dapper conservative dress that Amy had goggled, tempted to laugh aloud, but then she'd seen the corresponding lessening of tension in the air and had appreciated the reason why he'd done it. It was obvious that he wasn't a doctor who concentrated solely on the disease process his patients were suffering, but considered the whole person as his charge.

'Well, then,' Mr Khalil said briskly, with a deliberately dismissive glance around the stark environment of this most clinical of surroundings, 'would you like to come upstairs to my domain? We have much better coffee and tea up there than they'll give you down here in A and E…and more comfortable chairs.'

A porter had obviously been detailed to wait outside the room, and at the consultant's signal Amy gestured for him to bring the wheelchair in for Jane.

'Thank you,' the young woman said to Amy as they were about to leave the room, offering her hand. 'You've been very kind. Very understanding.'

'Good luck,' Amy whispered, as she reached her other arm around the slender shoulders for a gentle hug, pleased to see that Jane's eyes were less haunted now that her dreadful secret was out.

'I don't know whether luck will have anything to do with it, but I'm determined to live beyond my fortieth birthday, just out of sheer cussedness,' she said with an unexpected grin. Amy frowned, not understanding the significance, but Francis laughed aloud, an unexpectedly joyous sound in the previously sombre atmosphere.

'That's been a joke between us for years,' he explained. 'We have this agreement that when she gets to her fortieth birthday, for one day only I will have the option of a "two for one"—with her agreement, I can swap her for two of twenty.' He swallowed hard to regain control of his suddenly shaky voice, his eyes shiny with the threat of tears as he gazed lovingly down at her. 'It looks as if she's determined to veto the swap and keep me for herself.'

Amy was busy for the next half-hour, making certain she'd caught up with all the outstanding paperwork on the patients she'd seen during that shift and flagging any outstanding tests and investigations for the next shift to chase. But suddenly work was over for the day and she suddenly realised that something had changed inside her.

'It was the Paxmans,' she murmured, as she leant back against the wall in the changing room, her discarded scrubs dangling from one hand. In her mind's eye she could see the loving way Francis had cradled his wife and cried over her distress. *'That's* what I want in *my* life.'

And what had she got at the moment? The threat of a diagnosis of cancer hanging over her head, an ongoing battle with parents unwilling to let her live her own life and a something-and-nothing relationship with the man who'd stolen her heart when she'd been nothing more than a teenager.

'It's time to start sorting things out,' she said aloud, a new determination flooding her with energy for the task ahead. It was either that or she'd explode with unresolved tension.

The shrill sound of a pager intruded on her thoughts and she realised with a chuckle that she'd just thrown it in the basket with her scrubs.

'They're out of luck. I'm off duty,' she gloated, then shrugged fatalistically as she reached for the nearby phone, unable to ignore the summons.

'Amy Willmott here. You paged me?'

'Dr Willmott, you have a visitor at Reception.'

'A patient?' Amy queried, wondering why the reception-ist wouldn't just have directed whoever it was to triage or the nearest on-duty staff.

'No. Not a patient.'

Suddenly she realised who it must be. Her father…or perhaps both of her parents, finally tiring of playing telephone tag with her answering-machine. Well, perhaps it was a good thing that this was going to happen on more or less neutral ground because this time she wasn't ducking the confrontation. She loved them dearly but it was time to lay down some ground rules.

'Shall I show them to the relatives' room?' asked the voice on the phone, and Amy agreed.

'Please. And could you tell them I'll be with them in a couple of minutes?' It shouldn't take her any longer than that to drag a brush through her hair and swipe her mouth with a touch of colour. It wasn't as if she needed to impress them. 'Oh, and some clothes might be a good idea!' she exclaimed when she caught sight of herself in the mirror. 'More haste, less speed!'

But she couldn't help being in a hurry to get her life on track again. Ever since Edward had been killed, she'd felt almost as if she was drifting aimlessly, her emotions put on hold, but that was about to stop.

'There's nothing like having a diagnosis of cancer hanging over your head for making you realise what's really important,' she declared aloud, suddenly not caring if anyone could overhear her.

CHAPTER NINE

AMY pushed open the door to the relatives' room and stopped in her tracks when she saw not her parents waiting for her but a pretty young woman with a fretful baby in her arms.

'Can I help you?' she asked, struck by the feeling that there was something familiar about the young mother's face.

'Dr Willmott, you probably won't remember me but I'm Sharon Lees. I used to work in Theatre with your husband and…and…'

Without any warning, she burst into tears, her sobs only seeming to intensify the wails of the child in her arms.

Amy had no idea what had brought the young woman here to find her, but recognised that she needed time to get herself under control.

She heaved a silent sigh, realising that it was going to be some time yet before she left work, and held out her arms to relieve the young woman of her unhappy burden.

'You look exhausted, Sharon. Sit down while I see if I can rustle up a pot of tea. I won't be a moment.'

By the time a tray of tea and biscuits had been rustled up and delivered, she'd somehow managed to soothe both mother and baby by concentrating on them as if they were distressed patients.

'So…' she began, hoping they could get to the point fairly quickly once Sharon had managed to mop her face and take several sips of tea. She needed to go and speak to her parents to clear the air before she could see Zach and tell him what was in her heart. Anyway, people could be needing this room at any time so she would start with the obvious. 'You wanted to see me, Sharon?'

'I just didn't know what else to do,' she whispered, tears welling in her eyes again. 'I know none of it's your fault. Edward explained right at the start that the two of you had an open marriage and you didn't mind that he…'

Amy was so shocked by the matter-of-fact assertion that she was completely speechless. An *open* marriage? she repeated silently with a fierce surge of anger. Edward had actually told this young woman that his wife was *happy* that he was being unfaithful? He'd implied that she was betraying her vows, too?

Everything inside Amy was revolted by the idea and suddenly she knew such rage that if Edward hadn't already died on that motorway she'd have… Ooh! She had no idea what she'd do, or say. She only knew that the blinkers were well and truly off now.

'I know I wasn't the first person he'd had an affair with,' Sharon hurried on, while Amy bit her tongue, knowing that nothing was to be gained by haranguing the already distraught young woman. 'But when I discovered I was pregnant…' She looked up at Amy as she swayed gently to soothe the baby, the warm little bundle apparently happier now that it was settled against her shoulder. 'I half hoped he might want…' She shrugged and heaved a jagged sigh. 'He was making all the arrangements for me to have an abortion when he died, but somehow I couldn't kill his baby then. It just didn't seem right. But…I just didn't know how hard it was going to be, all on my own.'

'Can your family help you…do some babysitting so you can get out?' Amy probed gently, trying to divert more tears, but it was obviously the wrong thing to say.

'I haven't got any family any more,' she wailed, the tears flooding again. 'My dad died during my training—he was infected with MRSA when he went into hospital for a hip replacement—and my mum…well, she just faded away without him.'

Amy suddenly realised how grateful she was that she still had both of her parents, no matter how difficult it could be coping with their constant interference. She remembered, too, the way Edward's elderly parents had been visibly fading since they'd lost their precious son.

She remembered especially that the last time she'd visited them they'd said that it broke their hearts every day to remember that she hadn't been ready to give Edward the child he'd wanted so badly…the grandchild they'd never have.

Only her respect for their grief had made her bite her tongue and keep the truth to herself—that she'd actually been trying to persuade Edward that it was surely time to start their family, only to have him put her off yet again.

She cradled the little head in the palm of her hand and laid the little body in her arms so that she could look at that tiny face again.

'He's the mirror image of Edward, you know,' she said

quietly, remembering with an inward grimace the myriad photos and mementos of their son that had turned his parents' home into a veritable shrine.

'That's what I called him as soon as the scan told me it was a boy...Edward,' Sharon said, and an idea took instant root in Amy's head.

It was obvious that the older couple needed to know about Sharon and baby Edward every bit as much as the overwhelmed young woman needed their help. Amy had no doubt that their pleasure in discovering they hadn't completely lost their son would swiftly bury the fact that he'd casually broken his marriage vows.

It was the work of a moment to explain her idea and ask for Sharon's permission to phone the Willmotts—permission all too eagerly given—and even as she was contacting them to arrange an introduction in the least stressful way possible, Amy could feel a great weight lifting off her shoulders.

Silently she examined the feeling and realised that something that would have been devastating just a few short weeks ago barely warranted a ripple of regret. Edward was firmly in her past. She'd definitely moved on since Zach had come back into her life.

Was she angry that the man she'd married had been so casual about his vows? Yes, most definitely. Would she let it cast a pall over the rest of her life and stop her taking a chance that she could have something wonderful with Zach? No way!

By the time Amy waved Sharon on her way with an agreement to go with her for her first meeting with baby Edward's grandparents, she was exhausted, too. She certainly didn't need to emerge from the relatives' room to find her parents waiting impatiently to speak to her.

'Bring it on!' she muttered under her breath, as she led the way back into what was becoming her own personal space.

As the three of them waited stiffly for one tea tray to be replaced with another, Amy wondered idly whether some malign force had heard her determination to sort her life out and had decided to make her do it all at once.

Well, she may as well get as much of it over as she could while the resolution was fresh.

Her father waited just long enough for the social niceties to be observed, with each of them holding a freshly poured cup of tea that none of them bothered to taste, before he began.

'This just isn't good enough,' he declared, fixing her with his sternest glare. 'You certainly weren't brought up to be rude enough to ignore messages on your answering-machine. One can only assume that it's the company you've been keeping that has caused this serious decline in—'

'Enough!' Amy interrupted, with the same sort of force she sometimes had to use when they were inundated with drunken rowdies on a Saturday night. It worked just long enough to put him off his stride, but not for long.

'There you are!' he exclaimed. 'That's exactly what I mean—interrupting when your father's—'

'I said, that's enough, Father,' she repeated angrily, depositing her unwanted tea on the little table with a clatter and shooting to her feet to tower over him, her hands clenched into fists that had more to do with nerves than antagonism. 'I'm thirty-two years old. It's time you realised that you can't do this to me any more.'

154 A VERY SPECIAL PROPOSAL

'But, Amy, we're your *parents*,' her mother interrupted self-righteously.

'Yes. My parents,' Amy agreed. 'Not my jailers! I respect you both, and I'm grateful for everything you've done for me, but I don't need you supervising my every move any more. You're *stifling* me!'

'But if we see you making a mistake, it's our *duty* to stop you,' her father blustered with his usual conviction that he was unquestionably right. 'It's no different from when you were a teenager and had to work with that ne'er-do-well the first time.'

Amy blinked in astonishment. Working with a ne'er-do-well? Who on earth…?

'You mean *Zach*? Zach Bowman?'

'Of course I mean him,' her father snapped. 'He's trouble and always has been. I was on the board of governors of your school so I knew all about him. If the teachers could have found a way of getting him transferred to another school… That would've stopped him sniffing around you. You certainly shouldn't have had to be mixing with that sort of riff-raff.'

'*Riff-raff?*' she echoed, incensed. 'He became a doctor, the same as I did, Father. Does that make *me* riff-raff, too?'

'And that's another thing,' her father interrupted, ignoring her question as irrelevant. 'That boy was so thick that there's no way he could be a doctor…not legally. I fully intend to instigate an inquiry into the hospital's policies for checking up on applicants' references. Can you imagine what the press would make of it if it was uncovered that we'd employed an unqualified doctor in the A and E department?'

'*No!* Father, if you *dare* to do that, I will *never* speak to you again!' Amy said through gritted teeth, horrified that he could even think of such a thing and barely restraining herself from screaming with frustration. What he was proposing doing could utterly destroy Zach's reputation. 'Zach is *not* thick and never has been. He's dyslexic.'

'He's what?' At least that medical-sounding term had stopped her father in his tracks for a moment.

'He's dyslexic, but that doesn't stop him being extremely bright…which he is…or a superb doctor…which he is, too. And… What did you mean when you said he'd been 'sniffing around' when I was a teenager?' Her father's assertion had finally penetrated the haze of anger surrounding her brain but she certainly couldn't remember any occasion when one of her contemporaries had dared to invite her out, least of all Zach. They had all been too much in awe of her powerful father to chance it.

'Just what I said,' he said shortly. 'The arrogant pup actually came right to our front door, wanting to talk to you about taking you to some dance or other. So I told him you wouldn't be interested. You were just months away from going to medical school. The last thing you needed was to get involved with some local yob. And I was right,' he crowed in self-satisfaction. 'You met Edward and—'

'Edward!' she exploded, flinging both arms up in the air. 'Oh, yes, I met Edward, your perfect, precious Edward.' She snorted when she saw their open-mouthed shock at her outburst. 'Let me tell you about a visitor I had just before you arrived this evening. She's a young nurse who came all the way here to say that she knew that Edward and I had an open marriage and that she certainly wasn't the first person he'd had an affair with, but…just before he died, she discovered that she was pregnant.'

There wasn't a peep out of either of her parents now. They were staring at her positively goggle-eyed with shock.

'And so, my wonderful husband Edward, of whom you were so proud, was going to organise a speedy abortion to get rid of his unfortunate little mistake, but then he died and she couldn't bear to get rid of the baby. Unfortunately, she never realised it was going to be so hard, coping on her own, because she hasn't got any close family left.

'And then I remembered how upset Edward's parents had been that they were never going to have a grandchild now because I hadn't been ready to give Edward the child he'd wanted so badly.'

That jolted her mother visibly. Amy had actually confided to her that she'd been trying to persuade Edward that it was surely time to start their family, only to have him put her off yet again.

'Only my respect for their grief made me bite my tongue and keep the truth to myself, but this evening, when I saw that little boy, and how much he resembled Edward…'

'But we couldn't have known he would do that to you,' her mother pointed out weakly. 'We were only doing what was best for you.'

'So you say,' Amy conceded, needing to draw this draining meeting to a close before she collapsed with exhaustion. She needed to stay strong because any hint of weakness would give them the excuse to take over again. 'But you had your chance at organising a perfect life for me, and I ended up with a womanising husband who was more interested in climbing the career ladder as fast as possible than in spending time with me or starting a family. So, now it's *my* turn.'

'So, what *are* you going to do?' her father demanded belligerently. 'Not spend time with that—'

'Father, I don't intend discussing it with you because it's none of your business,' she interrupted firmly. 'You are free to offer me as much advice as you like, but I am every bit as free to ignore it. I will go out with whomever I please, and if at some time in the future I decide to marry again, I promise to let you know in time to send your suit to the dry-cleaner's and for Mother to buy a new hat. Other than that, my private life is just that—private. Now, if you don't mind, I went off duty nearly two hours ago and I'm due to meet someone in about half an hour.'

'If it's that…' her father began, only to subside when her mother gave him a totally uncharacteristic dig in the ribs with her elbow to silence him, before rising elegantly to her feet.

Amy gave each of them a hug as she ushered them out of the room but, as usual, it was barely more than a brushing of cheeks with her mother, out of deference for her immaculate make-up, and was accompanied with a fulminating glare from her father.

'Well, that went swimmingly,' she muttered wryly, as she thrust her arms into her jacket and retrieved her keys. Her expression lightened when she remembered that tonight was when Zach had suggested taking her ice-skating…before he'd started avoiding her. Now, full of new determination, she was going to call on him at home, using that original invitation.

They may not have had any long heart-to-heart talks about their feelings towards each other, but she certainly knew that there was *something* there between them, something that had its origins in a science lab all those years ago. All she had to do was go to him and find out if there was any possibility of a long-term relationship…whether he could love her as much as she loved him.

Her brain was still on overload as she began driving around the car park, joining the steady stream of cars trying to exit onto the busy road at the main entrance.

'Could anything *more* be crammed into a single day?' she mused aloud then chided herself. 'Bite your tongue, Amy. Whenever anyone in A and E says something like that, it's the signal for all hell to break loose!'

But it had been fraught, right from the moment she'd opened that letter that morning. And it still wasn't over yet. She desperately needed someone to talk to while she was waiting for the results of the second collection of cells and the thought of confiding in her mother…well, it just wasn't an option. Not only did she want to spare her mother the worry, they just didn't have that sort of relationship. In fact, the one person she felt that she could really pour her heart out to was Zach.

As if thinking about him was enough to make him appear, there was a familiar scarlet motorbike roaring towards her along the main road as she waited for the traffic to clear to allow her to emerge from the hospital's main entrance.

She was already smiling at the thought that she should be able to follow him all the way home when, out of the corner of her eye, she saw a car approaching from the other direction, going far too fast as it indicated that it was going to turn into the hospital entrance, apparently oblivious of any other road user.

As if in slow motion, she saw the car turn to cut right across the motorbike's path; saw the rider's frantic manoeuvres as he tried to avoid a collision; saw the bike veer towards her own car, then away again and finally lose traction on the rain-slick street to plough into the side of her car, just in front of her feet.

In spite of the fact that he'd been braking fiercely, the rider's momentum was enough to catapult him off the bike and send him cartwheeling over the front of her car to land with a sickening thud on the road.

'Zach!' she screamed, fighting to release her seat-belt even as she speed-dialled the emergency number to report an accident right outside the hospital's main entrance, then having to fight to open her door, the hinges obviously deformed by the force of the impact.

It seemed to take far too long for the call to go through and for ever for her to reach his side…an eternity in which he could be bleeding to death or breathing his last breath. She couldn't bear to think about the possibility that his neck had been snapped or his skull shattered.

She should have spoken to him sooner, she thought with a flash of agony for missed opportunities. She should have told him that she'd fallen in love with him years ago…that she had never really stopped loving him since those days when they'd been partners in the science lab.

'Zach…' she whimpered, as she finally fell to her knees beside his crumpled form, hardly even daring to touch him in case she caused more injuries. She stripped off her suit jacket to lay it over him to protect him from the rain and was instantly soaked to the skin. 'Can you hear me, Zach? Can you talk? Where does it hurt?'

She desperately wanted to cradle him in her arms but she daren't move him or even touch his helmet in case she paralysed him. At least the ambulance didn't have far to come and then he'd be in safe hands.

'Everywhere!' The word was muffled by his helmet and halfway between a groan and a growl as he gingerly moved first one arm then the other then tested each leg in turn. 'Help me sit up,' he demanded, and Amy's medical training finally overcame her emotional response.

'Don't you *dare* move anything else until you've been checked over properly,' she ordered fiercely, gripping his shoulder to prevent him disobeying her. 'If you've got spinal injuries, you could end up paralysed.'

'No chance of that, love.' He shrugged her hand off and rolled away from her, regaining his feet with a lithe economy of movement that totally belied the fact that he'd just been thrown off his bike at speed. He reached up with one hand to flip up the visor on his helmet just as another voice reached her from the other side of the car park.

'Amy! My God, *Amy*!' Her head spun to face the man racing across the hospital car park towards her in the familiar hospital scrub suit, his long legs moving so swiftly that his feet barely seemed to touch the ground.

'Zach?' She would know that voice anywhere.

Bewildered, she turned back to the man now looking down at her from the confines of his helmet to see unfamiliar pale grey eyes returning her gaze.

'Mistaken identity?' he queried lightly. 'Sorry to have given you such a fright but it honestly wasn't deliberate.' He grimaced towards his bike, now embedded up to the front forks in the side of her car. 'I wouldn't do that to a decent bike on purpose—unless I was being paid for it.'

'Paid for it?' Amy parroted with a frown, her brain obviously not processing information properly after such a shock. She'd honestly believed that it was Zach's bike and that he...

'It's my job,' her patient explained, and she could just see the attractive crinkles at the corners of his eyes that told her he was smiling inside his helmet. 'I'm a stuntman. Josh Harnett. Pleased to meet you.' He held out a gauntleted hand then drew it back to take the tough leather glove off and offered it again.

'And you,' Amy responded rather incoherently, automatically noting that Zach had nearly reached them, his scrubs already drenched by the steady rain and clinging to him like a second skin. She forced herself to concentrate just a moment longer, holding onto his hand for emphasis. 'But, please, I don't care if you do this sort of thing on a daily basis, *please* go into the A and E department and let them check your neck and your head before you take that helmet off.'

'Anything for you, beautiful lady with the once beautiful car,' he teased, charm personified, but it had absolutely no effect on her pulse rate, unlike the man sprinting towards her.

'Amy! Are you all right?' Zach demanded when he reached her, his chest heaving after his effort. His hands almost felt as if they were shaking as he held her by her shoulders, his dark eyes skimming over every inch from head to foot, looking for signs of injury.

'I'm fine, Zach,' she reassured him quickly, warmth flooding through her at this evidence that he cared whether she'd been hurt. 'My car protected me. It was Josh who bore the brunt of it, coming off and landing like that, but he's a—'

'Help us!' called a panic-struck male voice, and Amy suddenly realised that she'd completely forgotten about the occupants of the car that had caused the accident in the first place. As they hadn't been involved in the crash, she'd assumed that they had escaped unscathed.

'Are you hurt, sir?' she asked, striding swiftly across and bending down to peer inside the car, knowing that Zach was right behind her.

What she really wanted to do was give the crazy driver a piece of her mind for driving so dangerously that he'd nearly cost a man his life. If Josh hadn't been trained to know how to fall...

'My wife's in labour! Help her, please!'

Hysteria. Panic. Fear. They were all combined in the man's voice as Amy hurried to open the rear door of the car. There on the back seat, completely out of sight until this moment, his wife lay panting and moaning.

'Hello. I'm Amy and I'm a doctor,' she said reassuringly. She braced one knee on the edge of the seat to lean inside the car far enough for the woman to see her and to make a primary assessment. She was barely aware of the whoop of an ambulance arriving on the edge of the rapidly developing traffic jam at the hospital's main entrance. 'How long have you been in labour?'

'I'm Joyce and I don't *know* how long. I only had backache and then my waters broke and... It's coming! I can feel it!' She wailed suddenly and Amy saw the prominent bulge of her belly change shape as it grew hard with a contraction.

Taking her at her word, Amy started to reach into the car, only to have a hand—Zach's hand, she knew, without needing to look—grasp her elbow to stop her, reaching round her with the other to present her with a pair of disposable gloves, no doubt provided by the ambulance paramedic.

'Don't take any more chances,' he murmured in her ear, and for just a moment she allowed herself the luxury of feeling surrounded by warmth and concern before he was gone again.

Joyce moaned and it was time to act, but before she could snap the gloves in position and reach in to unceremoniously strip Joyce of her damp underwear, Zach was back again, literally covering her back to protect her from the increasing ferocity of the rain as he handed her a sterile towel to lay on the car seat under the woman's hips, followed by another to drape over her upraised knees to provide at least the semblance of modesty and privacy.

'You're right, Joyce!' Amy exclaimed when she saw the evidence in front of her. 'The baby's head is already crowning.' There wasn't going to be time to make any more preparations. This baby was in a hurry.

'Is that bad?' the poor woman panted as the contraction faded, wide-eyed with terror.

'Not at all,' Amy soothed. 'It's good. Very good. It means your baby's nearly here.' There certainly wasn't time to get her to A and E, let alone up several stories in a lift to a delivery suite. It looked as if it was up to her to make sure the little one arrived as safely as possible.

'Entonox?' Zach suggested, letting her know it was available in case the mother-to-be needed something to take the edge off the pain, but she was already pushing again, totally focused on bringing this precious new life into the world and clearly oblivious to any incidental suffering.

'Good girl!' Amy praised when the head emerged completely with the next long push, the little face screwed up into a disgusted grimace. 'Now, Joyce, can you stick your tongue out for me and pant like a dog for a minute?' she suggested, knowing that it would be almost impossible for the labouring woman to push with her mouth open like that. She needed enough time to check that the cord wasn't around the baby's neck before Joyce pushed again.

'Please…I want to push! I *need* to push!' she begged, just as Amy confirmed that all was well.

'Just a *little* push, Joyce,' she said, supporting the baby's head gently and allowing it to rotate naturally so that first one shoulder then the other emerged, swiftly followed by the slither of the rest of the body straight into her waiting hands.

'Here you are, Amy,' Zach said, his deep voice right beside her, his breath warm on the side of her face as he handed her a soft cellular cotton blanket to wrap the tiny body, its little mouth already opened wide in an angry wail.

'Thanks.' She glanced up at him as she took it from him and saw that his eyes were just as moist as hers were with the emotion of the moment. They didn't see very many deliveries in A and E, much less in the back seat of a car in the car park, but every one of them was special.

'You've got a little girl, Joyce,' she said with a smile as she laid the little bundle on her mother's stomach and guided her willing hands to hold her precious baby safe, knowing that her own part in this little drama was almost over. She would cut the cord to separate the two of them to make transporting them into the hospital easier, but the delivery of the afterbirth could be dealt with by more experienced staff now that the baby had been born and mother and child were safe.

'You two really *will* have to stop doing our job for us,' Harry complained, as the paramedic took her place at the open car door. 'Especially when it's the exciting things like delivering babies.'

'I'm sorry, Harry, but what can I say? If you're just too

slow off the mark to get there in time…' she teased as she stepped back to give him room, drawing off the gloves and dropping them into the bag Zach was holding open for her.

She smiled up into his dark eyes, and when she was struck by a sudden urge to trace his straight brows and lean jaw with her fingers and to stroke the sleek darkness of his hair, she realised that her feelings were now even more wired than they'd been when she'd left the hospital just…she glanced at her watch…well, it wasn't even half an hour ago.

She gave a shudder and suddenly realised that she was completely soaked to the skin.

'I know it was a factor in the accident, but I hadn't even registered that it was still raining,' she exclaimed in disbelief, bending to retrieve her sodden jacket from the roadway. It was only when she turned to make her way back to her car that she realised the full extent of her dilemma. 'Zach!' she wailed, 'I haven't even got any transport to get home!'

'I'm giving you a lift,' he said as though it was a foregone decision. 'Did you have any important errands you needed to do, or were you going straight home?'

She'd intended showering and changing her clothes and putting on fresh makeup before she drove herself over to his house for the next step in her 'Amy sorts her life out' campaign. Now she wouldn't have to.

'That's a bit academic, when we're both as wet as this!' Her laugh had a touch of hysteria as she gestured from her own suit—the third one she'd ruined recently—to the thin cotton scrubs plastered against his skin. 'The only place we need to go is into the nearest hot shower before we get pneumonia.'

She was looking directly up at him when she made the suggestion and saw the flash of desire that dilated his pupils, making his eyes look darker than ever. Her heart lifted at this evidence that he wasn't immune to the attraction between them either, and she was more determined than ever to find out whether there was any possibility of a long-term relationship between them.

'Doctor?' interrupted a female voice beside her, and Amy could have groaned aloud with frustration. 'If I could have a brief word?' the voice continued, and there was PC Frostic with a wry smile on her face. 'Hello, again. It doesn't look as if I'll be getting another chance to drive that gorgeous car,' she mourned. 'Have you got a local garage you want to contact to get it moved? Only it needs to be done as soon as possible so we can get the main entrance to the hospital cleared.'

'It's serviced at Greville's, if that's any help,' Amy offered, a bit at a loss over the organisation of such a situation as it had never happened to her before.

'They're good,' the policewoman said, 'but I can't see them being able to do much with it in that state. It looks like a write-off to me. The impact has probably turned the chassis into a banana.'

Amy had enjoyed her car, but just at this moment she really couldn't bring herself to care what happened to it. All she wanted to do was to grab Zach and hold onto him and to tell him that she loved him. Unfortunately, this was neither the time nor the place.

'I'm quite happy for you to do whatever you think best,' she said, trying to control her impatience. 'Will you need access to it for accident investigators to do their thing? I presume you'll be giving me an incident number so I can inform my insurers and they can do all the behind-the-scenes stuff.'

Why was she still here, babbling on about things that didn't matter a jot in the eternal cosmos, when the most important thing in her world was to go home with Zach and tell him she loved him?

'If Dr Willmott gives you *carte blanche* to do whatever you think best now, and she promises to do all the other legalities later, will that be all right?' Zach interrupted. 'Only she's been soaked to the skin for nearly an hour now.'

PC Frostic's eyes flicked from Zach to Amy and back again, and a hint of a smile tilted the corners of her mouth.

'I'm sure that will be quite all right, Doctor,' she said, and then the smile broadened just a little before she added softly. 'But we won't be contacting her until tomorrow, at least.'

And with that, their part in the whole emergency was over.

Any pedestrians had been driven away by the miserable weather as much as by the lack of anything interesting going on. The traffic was moving relentlessly on the nearby main road, while people wanting to enter or leave the hospital car park were being guided past the entangled vehicles one by one by a uniformed policeman.

Even the ambulance had gone, taking Joyce and her little daughter—her name changed to Amy in her novice midwife's honour—away up to the warmth and safety of the nursery.

'Are you ready to go?' Zach offered with a shiver of his own.

'Tell me you brought your car to work today,' she begged through chattering teeth.

He shook his head. 'It's the bike or nothing.' There was a

strange gleam in his eyes that set a thrum of excitement humming inside her.

'Like this?' she demanded, gesturing towards the blouse that was almost transparent when it was wet and knowing that he'd already noticed the effect that the cold water was having on her body. 'With you in your scrubs and me in a skirt again?'

'It's the only way to travel!' he teased, and lifted a questioning eyebrow.

As if her answer could be in doubt.

'All right, then,' she said, trying to sound resigned rather than excited by the prospect. 'If we're going to do it, let's get on with it before we both freeze to death.' Then she shrieked when he suddenly grabbed her hand and started running back across the car park towards his bike.

'Slow down!' she demanded, laughing too much to run properly.

'Can't. We need to run to get warm. And besides,' he added in a softer voice, almost as though talking to himself, 'we've already wasted enough time.'

CHAPTER TEN

ZACH felt Amy's slender arms wrap even tighter around him as he accelerated, her body leaning trustingly against his, and he swore aloud, glad that he hadn't taken the time to activate the intercom between the helmets.

He'd come so close to losing her that it didn't bear thinking about. Just a second or two sooner pulling out of the car park and that bike would have slammed straight into her, doing heaven only knew what damage.

And then, instead of a fit of the vapours after such a near miss, she'd calmly coached a terrified woman through the final stages of labour in the back of a car. Was it any wonder that she'd begun to occupy most of his waking thoughts…and all his dreams, too? If only there was some chance that there could be any sort of a future for them but, the situation being what it was…

'Put it plainly, man,' he muttered under his breath, as he swung the bike into the turn that would take him off the main road, revelling in the fact that Amy automatically leaned into it with him as though they'd been riding together for years. 'You can't deny that you first fell for her at school, or that she didn't feel the same way, otherwise she would hardly have enlisted her father to show you the door.'

And that had been after it had taken him weeks to screw his courage up to invite her to the school leavers' dance; weeks when he'd combined the endless hours of study necessary for him to have a chance of passing his exams with extra hours crammed in at the Friary each weekend to earn the money to hire the appropriate clothing. He could still remember the way Sheila and Melvin had shaken their heads and muttered under their breaths that he was burning the candle at both ends, the memory warming him with its evidence that they'd cared about him.

'Still, being knocked back had a good side,' he murmured, as he made the final gentle turn into his driveway. 'Not only did it permanently put me off getting involved with people beyond my means, but it made me more determined than ever to qualify as a doctor, so I suppose I should be grateful.'

Anyway, in spite of the fact that he'd succeeded against all the odds and was hopefully heading towards his consultancy, the situation between Amy and himself was essentially no different to what it had been all those years ago. She was still the princess to his pauper because, no matter how far up the career ladder he climbed, her social set would never accept him. He would always be the loser from the wrong side of town.

It was time he accepted reality, he lectured himself silently, even as he revelled in the touch of Amy's hands around his waist. Fooling himself that he'd been given a second chance with her was nothing more than that…foolishness.

Apart from anything else, *he* was the reason why her relationship with her parents was in a mess, because they *knew* he wasn't good enough for her, and that was the bottom line.

The logic of his thoughts made him cold to the bone but it was the result of the passage of air over his inadequate clothing that had chilled him so that it was difficult to reach forward to switch off the engine. Not that he was in any hurry to do so, with Amy huddled tight against him, perhaps for the last time.

He finally turned the key and removed it and the world became blissfully silent, until he removed his helmet to hear the convulsive chattering of her teeth.

Cursing himself under his breath that he hadn't thought to put her in a taxi instead, he quickly disposed of her helmet then scooped her up into his arms, smiling wryly at the romantic image it would present to anyone watching.

'I can w-walk!' she exclaimed, even as she threw her arms around his neck and clung to him.

'You're frozen stiff and it's quicker this way,' he countered unsteadily, unable to take his eyes off the long length of perfect legs draped over his arm, her skirt still trapped around her hips from the journey. And, anyway, he was enjoying the feeling of having her in his arms, her slender body now plastered against the front of him instead of his back. It was a small enough indulgence to store in his memory for all the days to come.

There were plenty of regrets stored away in there already. Impossible fantasies such as having her in his bed with that wealth of honey hair spread out across his pillow as she beckoned him to join her, while knowing that it would never happen, and more simple ones such as the fact that he'd never danced with her.

And she felt so right in his arms, he realised as he regretfully lowered her feet to the floor in the quiet warmth of his hallway. He'd held onto her for as long as he could, juggling keys and doors until the last possible moment just because it felt so good.

'Will you come dancing with me one day?' he blurted out, and could have bitten his tongue off when he saw the startled expression on her face. That brought him to his senses quicker than a slap and he could feel the heat of a teenager's blush flooding its way up his throat and into his face as he turned away.

'Forget I said that,' he muttered, mortified that he still couldn't get it right even after all these years. 'Wrong place, wrong time.'

Wrong man, he added to himself as he headed rapidly towards the kitchen to switch on the kettle.

'Zach?' Amy hastily called him back when it looked as if he was going to leave her standing there, her thoughts in complete turmoil.

Had he really asked her to go dancing with him, after all this time?

It was something she'd dreamed about and woven into her fantasies for so many years, but it had taken him just as many years to ask, so that she'd almost given up hoping. Hearing the actual words had taken her completely by surprise.

When she'd called his name he'd stopped walking away from her, but it wasn't until he reluctantly turned back towards her and she saw the expression on his face that she realised how much her apparent hesitation must have hurt him.

'I'd love to go dancing with you, Zach…if you meant the invitation?' Her heart was pounding and she hardly dared to breathe as she waited for his reply.

'What changed your mind?' he demanded stiffly, the expression in his eyes hidden, as ever, by those lowered lashes. 'I'm still the same Zach Bowman I always was—the rebel from the wrong side of town with hardly two pennies to rub together. I'll never be in your social class, as your father kindly pointed out.'

'My father?' It must be the cold that was making her brain work so slowly because she really couldn't understand what he was talking about. *When* would her father have spoken to Zach? She'd seen her parents leave the hospital just before she had, and they certainly hadn't spoken to him then.

He gave a cynical laugh. 'Surely you haven't forgotten? The time I asked you to a dance—the school leavers' dance—and you delegated your father to turn me down. He probably didn't do it quite as delicately as you would have face to face, but he left me in no doubt that you wouldn't welcome any further invitations from me.'

'The school leavers' dance...?' It was unbelievable that she'd only been thinking about that just days, or was it hours ago. 'I didn't know!' she exclaimed breathlessly, as surging joy that he'd actually wanted to go with her warred with bitter disappointment that her father really had interfered.

His expression told her he didn't believe her and she hurried towards him, words tumbling out of her mouth as she tried to find the right ones to convince him.

'I *did* want to go with you, Zach,' she insisted urgently. 'I was dropping hints about it for weeks. Don't you remember?' There was still no softening of his expression, or in the rigid muscles under her hand where she gripped his arm.

'Oh, for heaven's sake!' She flung both hands up in the air in exasperation and swung around to pace the length of his hallway and back. 'Can you honestly imagine me giving my father instructions to tell a potential dance partner never to darken my door? Surely you've realised what he's like—what *both* my parents are like with their outdated class consciousness and air of superiority. The only thing they're interested in is a person's social standing, not what they're like *inside*.'

He sighed and to her relief she saw the taut line of his shoulders relax. 'When you put it like that, it does sound rather…Victorian, doesn't it?' he admitted ruefully. 'And it would tie in with what was going on at that fundraiser when you shanghaied me into getting you out of there, and—'

'Oh, if only you'd asked me before we left school. My father would never have had a chance to interfere!' she exclaimed, and something in his expression made her ask the obvious question. 'Why didn't you?'

'Male ego,' he admitted wryly. 'I didn't dare do it at school in case you turned me down in front of all those witnesses. I thought that if I went to your house, I could ask you on your own.'

'And, instead, got my father,' she said, with a convulsive shudder that had everything to do with sodden clothing, chilled flesh and exhaustion.

'Dammit, what on earth are we doing, yakking down here when you're freezing?' he said, when he saw her nearly topple off her feet.

'It's not just the rain,' she explained, as he ushered her solicitously up the stairs then led the way towards the bathroom. 'Almost as soon as I finished my shift, I had a couple of visitors.' She gave an abbreviated version of the bombshell Sharon Lees had delivered.

'It was *Edward's* baby?' He'd stopped so abruptly that she nearly ploughed into his back and his expression was almost murderous when he turned to face her.

'It couldn't have been anyone else's,' she said with a wry smile. 'The resemblance to his baby photos was uncanny.'

'And…how do you feel about…?' He shrugged.

'Relieved, if you want the truth,' she admitted bluntly, hoping she hadn't shocked him. 'It was very hard, living up to the image, and now I don't have to any more.'

'The image?' He'd leaned back against the wall and with his face partly shadowed she couldn't see his expression well enough to judge what he was thinking. Not that it would make any difference, because she wasn't going to hide her thoughts and feelings any more.

'That I had to be the perfect grieving widow of the perfect cardiothoracic surgeon who died a hero when, in fact, all I was really grieving for was what I *hadn't* had.'

'Such as?' he prompted.

'Such as a husband who didn't value me for anything more than my good blood lines and the way they would help him up the career ladder. Such as a real home where you could curl up with a box of chocolates and a good book rather than a picture-perfect residence where the style police could visit at any moment without finding a single fault. Such as a family that didn't have to wait until all its father's ambitions had been fulfilled before it could come into being.'

Zach slowly shook his head and a laconic smile tilted his lips. 'The man was a fool not to realise what he had,' he said softly. His eyes were caressing her as they took a leisurely journey over her face, lingering at her mouth until she couldn't help the flick of her tongue moistening them in subconscious invitation.

She saw him swallow, his throat moving convulsively in response, and she heard the husky groan that followed as he dragged his eyes away and straightened up abruptly.

'The bathroom is between the two bedrooms, accessible from both,' he said raggedly. He pushed open the door beside him to reveal a room that Amy instinctively knew was his, with its minimalist decor and the clean lines of the pale wood furniture. The colours ranged from ivory through toffee to dark chocolate and was an invitation to relax and unwind…except relaxing was the last thing on her mind when she watched Zach's long-legged stride taking him to the door on the opposite side of the room, and she realised that his scrubs were still delineating that powerful body to perfection.

'You can have the first shower while I go and make us a hot drink. Which would you prefer, tea or coffee? Or I might even have some hot chocolate lurking at the back of a cupboard. There are plenty of clean towels in the cupboard and…' His voice died away when he turned and caught sight of the tears that had suddenly appeared from nowhere to trickle down her face.

'Amy? What's the matter?' There was a touch of panic in his voice and she shook her head.

'Nothing,' she said with a shaky smile. 'Nothing *now*, but I just remembered how it felt when I thought that was *you* lying there in a crumpled heap in the road.'

He drew in an audible breath. 'It was probably something like the way I felt when I saw that bike smash into the side of your car.'

Their eyes met and clung as they each re-lived those moments of terror, speaking without any need for words about their mutual fear, each believing that the other had been seriously injured…even killed.

'I should go…let you have your shower,' he said, even as his eyes told her that he couldn't bear to let her out of his sight.

'Don't go,' she whispered, her feet carrying her to him without her having to think about it, the need to be with him so great. 'Share it with me…'

His eyes widened as her words registered, and she saw him swallow abruptly.

'Do you mean it?' he demanded hoarsely, then shook his head. 'What am I thinking? Of course you don't. It's just because you're overtired after a busy day, then there was the shock of finding out about Edward, then you were nearly killed and had to deliver a baby…'

'And the only thing that matters,' she said softly, when his jerky litany ground to a halt as his eyes followed her fingers as they trembled their way through the row of buttons on the front of her blouse, 'is that I was terrified that you were dead and you were terrified that I was dead and we need to celebrate the fact that we're both very much alive.'

'And you won't regret…?' She silenced him with a fingertip on the lips she'd been fantasising about for ever.

'The only thing I'll regret is if you don't turn that shower on and share it with me,' she whispered, and replaced her finger with a teasing kiss.

It hadn't started out that way. Zach had been determined that what she needed most was a long hot shower to warm her to the core, but then she'd tempted him with a single kiss and it had exploded into something that warmed them both far faster than any shower.

'No…stop!' he ordered suddenly when she was convinced that he was every bit as eager as she was to start living the fantasy.

'Stop?' Her heart plummeted. It was the last thing she'd expected him to say.

'I don't want our first time to be like this,' he groaned, even as his arms tightened around her to demonstrate just how perfectly their bodies matched. 'I haven't put the new shower in and I don't want it to be hurried because the hot water might run out and we'll get frozen again.'

'So, does that mean there'll be a second time?' she asked, sliding against him provocatively.

'Oh, yes,' he growled, as he swung her up into his arms and stepped out of the cramped cubicle. 'And every other time,' he added, and it sounded like a promise.

We could have had this for years, if my father hadn't interfered, she thought with a brief flash of bitterness, then she dismissed such negative thoughts from her mind—they had no place there when this was the start of the rest of her life.

Like a bolt of lightning from a clear blue sky, she remembered the result of the Pap smear hanging over her head and it was her turn to call a halt, even though he was using his hands and his mouth to drive her nearly mindless with pleasure.

'Zach…please…I need to talk to you,' she pleaded urgently, having to grab both his hands in hers to stop his mind-blowing attentions to her quivering body.

'Talk?' he rasped in disbelief, and she closed her eyes, cursing the fact that she hadn't thought about this sooner. She felt him drag in a steadying breath and then he dropped his head down until his forehead was pressed against hers. 'All right.' He blew the breath out in a steady stream that did nothing to cool her arousal. 'But can you talk fast?' he begged in a pathetic voice that nearly made her abandon the attempt.

Except the topic was such a serious one that joking had to be put aside.

'I don't really know where to begin, so bear with me.'

'We're already as naked as we're going to be,' he growled under his breath, then lifted his head to give her an apologetic smile. 'Sorry about that, but when you've been fantasising about something for this long…'

He shrugged apologetically but it was something that Amy had desperately needed to know, that he'd been fantasising about her, too. She'd never dreamed that she would meet someone like him…to meet *him* again, in fact, and find that he was the perfect person to complement her in so many facets of her life.

They enjoyed each other's company, even doing something as simple as eating take-away fish and chips, and he'd definitely managed to tease her out of her comfort zone, letting her fulfil her fantasy of riding behind him on that powerful machine of his. He even made the manic pace of their work in A and E feel better—more fulfilling—and he made her feel bold enough to think about trying new things, but…but she was dreading the next few minutes.

'I had…' she croaked nervously, and had to clear her throat and start again. 'I had a letter this morning about a cytology result,' she began, in danger of hyperventilating as she searched for the right words.

'About one of the patients?' He frowned, clearly confused as to why she would bring such a topic up now, while they were…

'No. About me,' she clarified, then blurted out in a rush, 'It said that my Pap smear result was ambiguous and they needed to repeat it.'

His arms tightened around her but his voice was calmness itself. 'So, have you made an appointment? Of course you have.' He answered his own question as though it was obvious. 'When are you having it done?'

'I had it done today,' she confirmed. 'Now I just have to wait for the results.'

While she'd been speaking he'd drawn his head back just far enough so that he could make eye contact with her, this time making no attempt to shield what he was thinking with the thick screen of lashes he'd used as a teenager. A small silence stretched out between them, as though he was waiting to see if she'd finished what she wanted to say, then he broke it with a strangely musing tone.

'I'm glad you wanted to confide in me, glad you felt you could, but…' He shook his head and deliberately cast his eyes down at the two of them naked. 'Why now?'

'Isn't it obvious?' she pleaded, feeling the sudden hot press of tears threatening and all the nightmare scenarios came tumbling out. 'Until I get the results, I won't know whether I've got cancer. I won't know whether I'll need an operation, or chemo or…'

'Or what?' he challenged softly, silencing her frantic words with a finger on her lips. A gentle caressing finger that went on to stroke its way through her hair, winnowing it out until it fanned around her head on the pillow. 'Or whether I'll want to have anything to do with you if you *have* got cancer? Is that why you stopped me from making love to you?'

'No… Yes…' Her breath caught and the tears were that

much closer to returning and getting harder to fight. Had she come this close to having everything she'd ever wanted, only to have it snatched away?

'Well, if that was the only reason why you stopped me fulfilling my most precious fantasy, then it's a particularly poor one,' Zach said in a fierce growl. 'I've loved you ever since that first titration we did together in the science lab, and nothing—not ambiguous Pap smears, cancer, chemotherapy or the imminent obliteration of the universe—is going to stop that. So, if you don't mind, I need to find my place again and continue where we left off.'

Disbelief. Joy. Relief. There were too many emotions flooding through her for her to make sense of them when the only one that really mattered was love.

She knew her smile was trembling a little but there was no hesitation when she wrapped her arms tightly around him.

'I think you were here,' she whispered, and tilted her head for the first kiss of the rest of her life.

Somewhere in the distance a phone was ringing, but Amy was so warm and comfortable and only just emerging from the most wonderful dream that she really didn't want to open her eyes and dispel it.

'Zach Bowman,' rumbled a voice in the depths of the chest under her ear, and her eyes flew wide to discover that it had been far more than just another ephemeral dream. She really *was* in Zach's bed, wrapped in his arms, and they really *had* made…

'Fantastic!'

…love together last night.

It was a short call but she could tell that it was one that was putting a smile on his face. She could hear it in his voice.

'What?' she demanded as soon as he put the phone down.

'That was PICU. Davey's regained consciousness!' Zach announced with a broad grin.

'Oh, thank goodness!' She chuckled. 'I think his sisters dragged him out of it. They've been relentless, talking to him, getting their mother to read to him *and* enlisting Dee and Jonno.'

That had been one of the unexpected results of the whole situation, the fact that Davey's mother had asked to be put in touch with the young couple to thank them for their help and kindness, and the friendship that had sprung up between them. Amy had also been gratified to learn that both youngsters had been making enquiries about possible medical careers.

Then Zach suddenly flipped her over and loomed over her with a purposeful expression on his face.

'Good morning, beautiful,' he whispered, but when she expected him to follow that up with a kiss he startled her by demanding, 'So, you enjoy riding on the bike?'

It took a moment for her brain to change gears.

'When I'm not soaking wet and inadequately dressed,' she agreed warily.

'Inadequately dressed,' he echoed softly, and his eyes darkened. 'That's another fantasy we might have to fulfil some time.'

'What fantasy is that?' She was already beginning to quiver deep inside. They'd already enacted a few and they'd only been together one night.

'Oh, you know the sort of thing,' he said airily. 'You, the motorbike and very few clothes,' he suggested wickedly, and she heard herself gurgle with delight.

'I like the way your mind works, Dr Bowman. Any other ideas?'

'How about that postponed trip to go ice-skating? That would give me an excuse to ogle those beautiful long legs of yours. Are you any good at it?'

'I've never tried,' she admitted, then grinned up at him. 'But going on last night's experience, we'll be spectacular at whatever we do together.'

'And even if we weren't, we'd have fun,' he pointed out, and she finally realised that he was deliberately teasing her and making her laugh to take her mind off the fact that her Pap smear result was hanging over her.

'What if I can't give you a child?' she demanded suddenly, the words bursting out of nowhere to startle her nearly as much as him. 'What if—?'

'Shh!' he soothed, combing his fingers rhythmically through her hair. 'We'll deal with that if it happens. Together. There are options and we'd decide which one is right for us…adoption…IVF…no children.' Then he cupped her face between those clever talented hands as if to make certain that she was looking straight at him when he continued, his unforgettable dark eyes absolutely calm and full of love.

'Amy, there's only one thing that is totally non-negotiable,' he declared seriously. 'You have to love me and I have to love you and we have to spend the rest of our lives together.'

'Mother. Father. We have something we want to tell you,' Amy said, as soon as the four of them were settled in the restrained opulence of her parents' sitting room.

'If it's about *him*…' her father began, with a glare in Zach's direction centred on their intertwined hands, only to subside just as swiftly when her mother shushed him with a glare of her own.

'Actually, it's about me,' Amy said, grateful for the supportive grip Zach had on her hand. 'I had to have a second Pap smear because the result of the first was inconclusive.' Her father's frown of incomprehension was almost amusing. Her mother's gasp and loss of colour wasn't. She clearly understood the significance, even if her husband didn't.

'Oh, Amy, why didn't you say something?' she demanded. 'Have you taken the second test? When will the results be through? Have they told you what the likelihood is that it's cancer?'

'Cancer?' her father repeated in shocked tones, for once the volume barely above a whisper. 'You've got…?'

'No. I haven't,' Amy told them firmly, the confirmation of her reprieve still overwhelming. 'I didn't want to tell you anything about it until I had the results, and they came through today. Apparently the original sample had been contaminated with blood, but the second one was completely clear.'

Zach had called her Machiavellian for coming up with this strategy, and had agreed that it would probably suit their purpose, but when she saw the tears of relief gleaming in both her parents' eyes, she felt quite guilty.

'Oh, Amy, thank goodness!' her mother exclaimed. 'You must be so relieved.'

'Very. If it had been positive, it might have meant that I'd never be able to have any children, and you'd never have been grandparents. As it is…' She paused significantly to meet Zach's loving gaze. 'Zach and I have decided that we want to get on with that project as soon as possible, so this is your warning to get your best suit to the dry-cleaner and buy a new hat, because you've only got a month to do it.'

'A month!' her mother gasped. 'You want to get married in a month? But that's not nearly enough time to get anything organised. Surely…'

'Mother, we've already been to see the registrar and fill in the forms,' Amy said, then added pointedly, 'We've waited fifteen years to be together and neither of us sees any point in waiting any longer. The cancer scare made us realise what was important.'

Zach cleared his throat and Amy saw the colour darken the lean planes of his face as he spoke. 'Mr and Mrs Bowes Clark, you don't have to worry about Amy. I love your daughter and I will spend the rest of my life making her happy. I hope you'll both be there to wish us well when we say our vows, but whether you are or not, we *will* be getting married in four weeks…'

'And we *will* be disgustingly happy for the rest of our lives,' Amy added with a wide, happy grin as words bubbled out of her. 'And if all goes well, we'll be making you grandparents approximately nine months after the wedding and hopefully at yearly intervals after that until we've got an absolute houseful, so we'll need some very hands-on grandparents to come over and read them bedtime stories and—'

'Amy?' Zach interrupted quickly, sounding almost panic-stricken. 'A new baby *every* year?'

'Well, perhaps we can negotiate that part as we go along,' she conceded cheekily. 'But my parents *have* been waiting a long time for the first one, and—'

'You leave us out of this, my girl!' her father decreed, apparently not certain whether to look disapproving or delighted by the sudden turn of events. 'That sort of decision is strictly between husband and wife.'

'But you will be there to wish us well?' Amy asked, tightening her grip on Zach's hand and feeling the answering pressure of his, steady and certain. He knew exactly how much it meant to her to have her parents' approval even though it would make no difference to their decision.

'Of course we'll be there,' her mother said with a tremulous smile. 'How could we not be there for the happiest day of your life?'